Unable to stop  **face and took l** 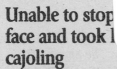 **cajoling**

The scent of baby powder lingered on her skin and she tasted like the banana she'd fed Dillon, sweet, delicious banana. He was drowning in it.

"Quinn..."

He touched her lips with his finger, not wanting to hear what she had to say because he knew it wasn't going to be in his favor. "Trust me, Britt. That's all I'm asking."

Trust me.

How could she do that?

In her heart, she knew she already had.

P9-BWS-246

Dear Reader,

For those of you who have written and emailed about Quentin Ross's story from *The Sheriff of Horseshoe, Texas*, this book is for you. Thank you for your many suggestions. I loved them all.

When I first started writing his story, I didn't see Quinn as a hero but when he saved Britt Davis from drowning, he became a hero in her eyes. And in mine.

There was a problem, though—Quinn didn't see himself as a hero, either. He was a hardnosed defense attorney focused on his career. That is, until he was pitted against Britt in a court of law. She changed his way of thinking, his life and his career.

So come along and find out how a regular man becomes a hero at the most wonderful time of the year.

Merry Christmas!

Love,

Linda Warren

P.S. It's the highlight of my day to hear from readers. You can email me at Lw1508@aol.com or write me at P.O. Box 5182, Bryan, TX 77805 or visit my website at www.lindawarren.net. Your letters will be answered.

Her Christmas Hero

LINDA WARREN

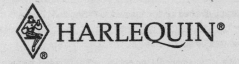

HARLEQUIN®

TORONTO • NEW YORK • LONDON
AMSTERDAM • PARIS • SYDNEY • HAMBURG
STOCKHOLM • ATHENS • TOKYO • MILAN • MADRID
PRAGUE • WARSAW • BUDAPEST • AUCKLAND

PLEASE RECYCLE · THIS PRODUCT IS RECYCLABLE

Recycling programs
for this product may
not exist in your area.

ISBN-13: 978-0-373-75337-6

HER CHRISTMAS HERO

Copyright © 2010 by Linda Warren

This edition published by arrangement with Harlequin Books S.A.

For questions and comments about the quality of this book
please contact us at Customer_eCare@Harlequin.ca

® and TM are trademarks of the publisher. Trademarks indicated with ® are registered in the United States Patent and Trademark Office, the Canadian Trade Marks Office and in other countries.

www.eHarlequin.com

Printed in U.S.A.

ABOUT THE AUTHOR

Award-winning, bestselling author Linda Warren has written twenty-six books for the Harlequin Superromance and Harlequin American Romance lines. She grew up in the farming and ranching community of Smetana, Texas, the only girl in a family of boys. She loves to write about Texas, and from time to time scenes and characters from her childhood show up in her books. Linda lives in College Station, Texas, not far from her birthplace, with her husband, Billy, and a menagerie of wild animals, from Canada geese to bobcats. Visit her website at www.lindawarren.net.

Books by Linda Warren

HARLEQUIN AMERICAN ROMANCE

1042—THE CHRISTMAS CRADLE
1089—CHRISTMAS, TEXAS STYLE
     "Merry Texmas"
1102—THE COWBOY'S RETURN
1151—ONCE A COWBOY
1226—TEXAS HEIR
1249—THE SHERIFF OF HORSESHOE, TEXAS

HARLEQUIN SUPERROMANCE

1167—A BABY BY CHRISTMAS
1121—THE RIGHT WOMAN
1250—FORGOTTEN SON
1314—ALL ROADS LEAD TO TEXAS
1354—SON OF TEXAS
1375—THE BAD SON
1440—ADOPTED SON
1470—TEXAS BLUFF
1499—ALWAYS A MOTHER
1574—CAITLYN'S PRIZE*
1592—MADISON'S CHILDREN*
1610—SKYLAR'S OUTLAW*

*The Belles of Texas

Acknowledgments

Thanks to Dottie Kissman and Phyllis Fletcher
for sharing their Austin. Thanks to Chris Pinada
for sharing her expertise of the courtroom.
And thanks to Lee Fay, pilot, for sharing his
expert knowledge of airlines.

Dedication

To my hero—Sonny

Chapter One

Stopping her vehicle on the flooded county road, Britt Davis knew she'd made a big mistake. Sheets of rain slashed at the windshield like an enraged warrior. Lightning lit up the sky and thunder rumbled with a dire foreboding. The wipers swished back and forth in frenetic motion, trying to ward off the blows—to no avail. The torrential downpour was winning the battle.

She peered over the steering wheel, searching for the road through the fury of the storm. All she could see was water and more water. The worn blacktop was fast becoming a lake. Fear clutched her throat and she flexed her clammy hands, gripping the wheel. Brushy Creek, known for flooding out of its banks, wasn't far away, and she had to be careful.

The shortcut to Taylor, Texas, from Austin seemed like a good idea thirty minutes ago. She had to get to her son. That was the only reason she was out in this storm. It had been four days since she'd held him, hugged him. Glancing at the papers lying on the passenger seat of her Camry, she knew she had to reach her baby as soon as possible. Her ex-husband had filed for temporary custody of their nine-month-old son, Dillon, on the grounds that he was the better parent, since her job as an international flight attendant took her away from their child for long periods of time.

Bastard!

Phil had been looking for a way to get back at her for divorcing him, and he'd found it. The only way to hurt her was through Dillon. She'd been served with the papers as she'd reached her apartment after a flight from Paris. Her mother, who lived in Taylor, kept Dillon while she worked.

Britt clenched her hands into fists. "Damn." Phil would not take her child.

Darkness fell like a heavy cloak as the October storm raged around her. Now her visibility was zilch as the warrior continued his assault. Rain pounded the car with a deafening sound. The headlights showed a watery path in front of her. She'd wait it out. That was all she could do.

Grabbing her purse, she reached for her cell to call her mother. She wanted to hear Dillon's silly giggles. She missed him so much. No signal. Her spirits sank lower. She needed to hear a friendly voice. Her head shot up as she felt the car move. *It couldn't!* She was imagining things. She peered through the swipe of wipers and saw the water on the road was rising. The wind whipped it fiercely against the car. Was she closer to Brushy Creek than she'd thought? Could…?

The thought froze in her mind as the car inched sideways, the wind and the water playing with it like a piece of flotsam. This wasn't her imagination. OhmyGod! No! No! This couldn't be happening. Another gust of wind and the car was swept into the rising waters. She screamed. But nothing stopped the nightmare. Her vehicle kept moving— swiftly. She had to get out. She had to get out of the car! If she didn't, it would be her grave.

Frantically, she undid her seat belt and reached for the

window button. It went down with a swoosh. Rain pelted her and water sprayed in. She screamed again, but sanity ruled. She had to keep her wits. As the car filled she fought against the splashing surge and pulled herself through the window, fighting to hold her breath, fighting for her life. The strong current took her slight frame and she struggled to keep her head up, to breathe. She had to stay alive—for Dillon.

Dillon!

The roar of the water filled her ears as its power swept her along. Her head went under and she swallowed putrid water, battling with everything in her to reach precious air. The current tossed her around like driftwood in the cold, dark night.

"Dillon," she called as her strength waned.

Suddenly her body hit an object and her frantic cry stopped. She was pinned against something. Gulping in air, she realized it was a log or part of a fallen tree. She wrapped both arms around the wet wood and tried to inch toward the bank, but the current kept pulling her back into the watery depths. Rain assaulted her eyes, blinding her. Plus it was so dark! How long could she keep up this battle? Terror gnawed at her heart and she shook, choking back a sob. The wind splashed murky slush against her face. As she grew weaker, hope of surviving seemed nil.

Giving in to nature wasn't in her plan, though. She did what she always did in a crisis. She prayed. Then she yelled at the top of her lungs, "Help! Someone please help me! Please!"

Her words mingled with the rain and the wind.

She weakened more and her arms slipped. No! She wouldn't give in. Wrapping herself tighter around the log, even though the bark cut into her skin, she kept yelling.

And praying.

QUENTIN ROSS WAS IN A hurry to reach Austin. He had a date with Deidre, and she didn't like it when he was late. He'd spent the day with his sister's family in Horseshoe, Texas. It was his nephew's first birthday and no way would he miss that. Peyton was happy with her husband and their two kids. She'd been domesticated, something he thought he'd never see from his pampered, flamboyant sister. These days she was still a little over the top, but that was Peyton, and always would be. But she didn't need pampering anymore, except from her sheriff husband, her soul mate, the right man for her. Watching all that love and family togetherness made Quentin wonder why he was still single at thirty-five.

Because the right woman always seemed to be wrong— wrong for him. Or maybe he chose the wrong women. His law career had been his top priority for years, but now he was feeling a pull for something else. His own family. He always had this feeling when he visited Peyton. Once he was back in the city, it would pass, he knew. There would be another case. Another person needing his help, and his focus would switch back to his career. Then there was Deidre....

She'd sliced and diced his heart so much it was a wonder it was still beating. But once again he'd agreed to go out with her—to talk. They rarely did much talking, though.

The rain was becoming intense and the strong wind tugged at his car. Damn! He should never have taken the shortcut to Texas 79, but he'd driven it many times before. Tonight, though, Mother Nature was bent on a rampage.

He reached Brushy Creek and saw that it was flooded out of its banks, the water swirling like a whirlpool. No way could he cross it. He'd have to turn around and find another way to Austin.

As he was backing up, his headlights flashed across

the swollen creek. Something bobbed in the water. What the hell? Was that a car? The driving rain kept him from seeing clearly, but it *looked* like the top of a sedan. Was someone in trouble?

He maneuvered his vehicle so his headlights pointed down the creek. Then he saw it—someone clinging to a log. Someone who needed help. He tried his cell, but the signal was weak. Without another thought, he opened his door and stepped out into the night. He was soaked to the skin in seconds, but didn't have time to think about himself. The person in the water needed help. Having been on the swim team in high school and college, he was a strong swimmer. He kicked off his shoes and dived in.

The cool water hit him like an electric shock, stealing his breath. It took a moment for him to get his bearings. The raging water bubbled around him and he tried floating with the current. But it was fierce, taking him quickly. He struggled to reach the person.

"Help me, please." The voice was faint. It sounded like a woman's.

"Hold on," he shouted, rain filling his mouth. He spit it out.

Finally he reached the log and grabbed on to the end, striving to keep his balance. From the way it wobbled he knew it was about to lose its anchor and drift downstream. "Don't let go," he yelled, inching toward the clinging figure while fighting the current. Coming up behind her, he placed his hands on the log next to hers, keeping her between his arms. At that moment, the log snapped. The flood took it for a ride, and them along with it.

"Don't let go," he said into her left ear, holding her close just in case she did.

"I…I…I…"

"Shh." He tried to calm her. "Just hang on. The log will stop soon."

The rain continued its brutal barrage and the flood-waters churned around them, along with the debris. Just when it seemed they were going to be washed away, the log caught on another fallen tree and stopped. Quinn knew he had to get her out of the creek now. Fighting the force of the wind and the rain, he urged her along the log.

When his feet touched the muddy bottom, he grabbed her around the waist and made for the shore, which was still about forty feet away. The water lapped at them, determined not to let go.

"Try to stand," he suggested.

"Oh, yes, I can touch the bottom," she replied, her voice excited.

"Don't stop. Keep going. We have to make it out of here."

They slogged through the mud and the water, trying to reach safety. At one point a monstrous wave caught her and she went down, flopping wildly. He snagged her and literally dragged her to the bank.

They lay in the mud, exhausted, the rain beating a steady tattoo on their backs. Then Quinn pushed himself up. "Can you stand?"

Without a word she staggered to her feet and followed him to higher ground.

"We have to go farther," he said raggedly. He couldn't see a foot in front of his face and had no idea what was out there. He just knew it was safer than the water.

Leading the way, he guided them into thick woods, into the darkness, into the unknown. Big trees with entwined branches lessened the stinging rain. He fell down beneath one. She huddled beside him as the storm raged on.

"THANK YOU," BRITT SAID when she could catch her breath. "I don't know what I would have done if you hadn't come along."

"What happened?" he asked, and she liked his voice—strong yet soothing, with a husky undertone.

"I was trying to reach Taylor and I couldn't see for the heavy downpour. I guess I was closer to Brushy Creek than I thought. The water just…just took my car." She couldn't stop the tremor in her voice.

"Are you okay?"

"I don't know. I feel as if I've been used as a punching bag." She wiped at her face. "Is it ever going to stop?"

"Eventually. Try to rest, and we'll walk to safety when it's daylight."

Rest? Was he kidding? She was wet and muddy from head to toe and her nerves were tied into knots. She might never rest again. Might never close her eyes again. But something about his voice, compelling and confident, lulled her into a calmer state. She wondered if he had that effect on all women when they were scared to death.

Taking a long breath, she let the knots ease. She was safe. She would see Dillon soon. But the rain tap-tapping on her head prevented her from sleeping.

"Did your car stall in the water?" she asked.

"No," he replied. "I was on my way to Austin. When I reached Brushy Creek, I could see it was flooded, so I turned around. As I did, I saw your car bobbing in the water and you clinging to the log."

Britt leaned forward, trying to see his face in the darkness. "So you jumped in?"

"Yes," he answered in a matter-of-fact tone.

Without any thought for his own safety? His own life?

How many men would do that? She didn't think there were any heroes left, but evidently one had just saved her.

"That was very heroic and dangerous."

"Mmm." He moved restlessly against the tree. "I'm not a hero. I saw you needed help and I didn't think about anything else. Later, when I've had time to think about it, I'll probably question my sanity."

"Well, thank you. My name is Britt."

"Short for Brittany?"

"No. Just Britt."

"Mine's Quinn. Now let's try to rest. Hopefully someone will be looking for us by morning. My car is parked on the road and someone will spot it. We just have to wait."

She settled beside him once again. "I hate that my mother will be worried."

"Is that where you were going?"

"Yes."

"Maybe she'll think you're waiting out the storm."

"Maybe." Britt closed her eyes and once again forced herself to relax. She was alive and Dillon was safe with her mother. Tomorrow she would set about putting her life back together.

The wind howled and the rain fell. The forest around them was dark, sodden and frightening. But complete exhaustion obliterated any panic. Without conscious thought, she rested her head on Quinn's shoulder and drifted into sleep.

With a perfect stranger.

BRITT WOKE UP TO A surreal feeling. She was wet, cold and disoriented. She hated nightmares, but this one felt so real. Her hand rested on something solid, hard—and alive, judging by the steady thudding beneath her fingertips.

She opened her eyes to an early dawn. A yellow glow

bathed the deep woods. The ground was soaked, as was she and the man sitting beside her. Who...? The night came rushing back with vivid clarity.

Dillon.

Her mother must be so worried. Luckily, Dillon was too young to know anything was amiss.

Britt was alive.

And the stranger who'd saved her was sleeping beside her.

She raised her head and stared at him. His drenched hair was slicked back and she guessed when dry it was a shade of blond. His face was all angles, with a jutting chin covered with a growth of dark blond hairs that gave him a sensual look. Long legs stretched out into the leaves. He had to be at least six feet or more, with a whipcord body made for rescuing damsels in distress.

When God was putting together heroes, he'd made this one perfect—brave and strong, with looks and character. The kind of man a woman would want beside her in sickness and in health, in youth and old age, and all the ups and downs in between.

She must have a concussion, Britt thought, touching her soggy, tangled hair. She'd sworn off men a long time ago—the day she'd come home and found her husband of six months doing drugs in their bedroom with a strange woman, naked. That had shattered all Britt's trust in men.

Why was she seeing such good qualities in this one? She didn't even know him. But what did she need to know? He'd risked his life to save hers. That was enough.

And it was good to know there were heroes. Maybe all men weren't scumbag jerks without moral fiber.

He stirred and she moved back on the wet ground, shiv-

ering. Not from fear, but the cold. For the first time she
realized she was chilled to the bone.

Yawning, he stretched his shoulders and opened his eyes.
A wave of warmth shot through her. His eyes were the most
beautiful color—sea blue, like she'd seen at the beach on
Padre Island. She wanted to dive right in.

"How are you?" he asked.

"Bruised, but happy to be alive." She gestured to the
forest. "It's stopped raining."

"Yeah." He swiped a hand over his hair. "I could use a
cup of coffee."

Glancing around at the thick woods, she said, "If you
find one out here, I'll fight you for it."

A stellar grin turned up the heat like a furnace. Charm,
too. The man had it all.

"You'd probably win. You're a fighter. Most women
would have let go of that log." He lightly stroked her black-
and-blue forearm. "That should heal in no time."

At his gentle touch a tiny jolt of pleasure lurched through
her and she lost her voice.

She wasn't a naive teenager. She'd been touched before.
What was wrong with her?

He rose to his feet in one lithe movement, his muddy
jeans and knit pullover clinging to him like a second skin,
emphasizing the taut muscles in his arms, legs and chest.
"Are you ready to start walking?"

"Uh...yes." She got to her feet rather slowly, and was
unprepared for the weakness in her legs. Her knees buckled.

Quinn quickly caught her before she hit the ground. His
arms were solid around her, and a telltale longing in her
lower abdomen weakened her even more. She hated herself
for that reaction.

To a stranger.

She pushed away. "Please don't touch me. I can stand on my own." Her voice was sharp, something she hadn't intended.

His blue eyes flared. "Excuse me."

Chapter Two

His eyes narrowed on her face and she wanted to take a step backward, but didn't. She'd made a fool of herself, so now she had to take her medicine, which was preferable to explaining how he made her feel.

"I'm not a helpless person. I can take care of myself." She heaved a breath. "I know it doesn't look like it. I made such a stupid decision coming out in the storm. Anyone else would have turned back. I feel like an idiot."

His eyes narrowed even more. "We've been through a harrowing ordeal," he finally said. "Let's push on." He turned and then suddenly swung back. "I was just trying to help you. It was a reflex. That's all."

"I know. I overreacted."

Quinn looked at her, really looked at her for the first time. Her eyes were dark, like the elderberry wine he'd drunk in college that had made him loopy. She probably had the same power to make men crazy. Long, provocative eyelashes framed her eyes. For a moment he thought they were artificial, but nothing about the woman said false. An abundance of dark hair hung in soaked strands around an oval face with defined cheekbones.

Bearing in mind her reaction to his touch, he tried not to stare at her body, but couldn't seem to look anywhere else. The mud on her face and clothes couldn't disguise her appeal. The sludge-coated jeans clung to her curves and the wet knit top left little to the imagination. The force of the water had ripped open three buttons and exposed the soft curve of her breasts.

The words *sex kitten* played through his mind, but were immediately replaced with *sugar and spice and everything nice*. He didn't know anything about her, but somehow sensed the latter fit her to a T.

A clap of thunder diverted his thoughts.

"Oh, no, not more rain," she cried.

"Looks like it. We better find some sort of shelter." As he spoke a fresh onslaught began to fall. "Let's go." He trudged through the deluge, with her a step behind him.

The weather was once again their enemy, and Quinn knew they couldn't continue to try to walk in it. Neither of them had shoes, and the ground was a muddy cesspool. He heard a cry and swung around to see that Britt had fallen headlong into the murky mess.

He rushed back to help, even though she probably didn't want it. Pushing to a sitting position, she wiped mud from her face. He couldn't tell if she was crying, but had a feeling she wasn't.

As he squatted beside her, he noticed some thick bushes around a tree. He pointed. "Shelter," he said above the pounding rain.

She climbed to her feet and he didn't offer assistance. Sloshing through the mud in his bare feet, Quinn reached the bushes and held back their wet branches so she could crawl inside. He quickly joined her. The thick yaupons offered some respite. A damp, musky smell surrounded them.

She shivered.

"Are you cold?"

"A little."

Without thinking, he put his arm around her. She didn't pull away as he expected, but nestled into him, their soaked bodies pressing together. Everything around them was wet, wet, wet, but an infusion of warmth eased through him just from holding her. Most women he knew would have crumpled into weeping hysteria by now.

"I feel like I'm in a nightmare," she murmured, tucking her head beneath his chin.

"Let's talk to get our minds on something else," he suggested. Lightning crackled in the distance, followed by booming thunder. Rain trickled from the branches on to them, but it wasn't bad.

"Men never like to talk."

"My mom says I was born talking."

"Are you close to your mother?"

"Kind of," he hedged, and wondered why. Maybe there were some things he didn't like to talk about.

"What does that mean?"

Before he could stop them, the words came pouring out, much like the rain—without warning. "When my sister and I were growing up, our mother worked for some very influential people in politics. She was gone a lot, running campaigns, doing whatever she needed to get a candidate elected. My dad raised us."

"But it worked for them, right?"

"On the surface."

This time Britt didn't ask what that meant. The rain drummed on, lulling him into a surreal state of mind. Sitting in the downpour holding her seemed natural. It wasn't, but it kept him talking.

"My dad was fifteen years older than my mother. They had a great deal of respect for each other and stayed together for the sake of their children." He paused. "Mom was very discreet about her affairs."

Quinn couldn't believe he'd told Britt that. He'd never even told Peyton. Maybe he needed to say the words out loud to rid himself of any lingering negative feelings.

"But they hurt you?"

He swallowed, and his throat felt raw. He had told his mother he understood, but he hadn't. Love wasn't supposed to be like that.

When he didn't respond, Britt turned her face to look at him. Her dark eyes were concerned, inviting confidences he somehow knew she'd never tell another soul. Being a defense attorney, he was good at judging people. He sensed she was a woman to be trusted. His instincts never failed him.

"I suppose," he murmured. "But we got through it. My dad died about seven years ago and my mom remarried. Life goes on."

The whirl of a helicopter interrupted him.

Britt sat up as well as she could in the confined area. "Is that…?"

"Hot damn. I believe it is, and it's stopped raining again." Neither had noticed while they were talking.

They scurried out like two squirrels and glanced toward the sky, which was barely visible through the weblike branches.

"They're searching," he said. "We have to find a clearing so they can see us." He took off through the trees and she followed.

The woods were thick and he held low limbs so they wouldn't slap her in the face. He didn't think twice about doing it; that was his nature. If she had a problem, then it was her own. But she didn't say a word and she didn't falter during their flight through the thicket.

When they finally came to a clearing, everything was quiet. The helicopter had moved on.

"Do you think it will come back?" she asked, an edge of desperation in her voice.

"They'll keep searching," he replied, staring at the gray sky.

She didn't panic or cry, and he liked that. She was strong, just as she'd said. But he wondered why she was so sensitive about being touched. The obvious answer was that some man had hurt her. With her pinup looks, he could imagine a lot of men losing their minds over her.

And he was getting into treacherous waters.

He'd had enough of that for one night.

Gulping a breath, he sank onto the damp grass. "We can wait here until it comes back. They'll probably make routine circles along the creek, checking for people in trouble."

"I hope so." She sat beside him. "My mother needs to know I'm okay. She's probably worried sick." Realizing her blouse was open, Britt pulled it together. "I feel like a drowned rat."

As she said the words, the sun poked through the clouds in a burst of warmth.

"Oh, my. Can you believe this?" She held her face up to it like a virgin worshipping the gods. "That feels so-o-o good." Tugging her fingers through her tangled hair, she tossed it about to help it dry.

He could only stare. He'd seen beautiful women before, but this one was different, and he didn't know why. *Real* came to mind. Natural. Fresh. And an aversion to being touched. That was like a rare piece of art never being seen or admired. Sacrilege, to his way of thinking.

Why he was thinking it at all surprised him.

After today, he'd never see the woman again.

He stretched out his legs in the drenched leaves, his bare

feet stinging from stepping on sharp sticks. Raising one foot, he rubbed it.

"How are your feet?" he asked.

"They're okay." She stopped fiddling with her hair. "But I don't think I'll ever get this mud out of my hair."

"Sure. Soap and water does the trick every time."

She cocked her head and seemed to relax a little. "So practical."

"That's me."

She twisted her body in discomfort. "I'm caked with mud. I've heard it said that mud wraps are good for the skin. Mine should be glowing."

His eyes traveled over the smooth lines of her face and neck. "It is." The words were in his head and it jolted him to realize he'd said them out loud.

Silence hung between them for a few seconds and a tell-tale shade of pink crept under her skin. "I get my olive complexion from my mom and grandmother. My grandmother is part Italian and part Polish, and has a fiery temper."

He raised his knees and rested his forearms on them. "Do you have a temper, as well?"

"Not really. I'm more like my father. It takes a lot to make me angry." Her eyes darkened.

"From the look on your face, I'd say someone in particular makes you angry."

"My ex." She picked mud from her jeans with a broken fingernail.

"Ex-boyfriend or ex-husband?" Quinn didn't know why he was inquiring about her personal life. Had to be the lawyer in him, he told himself. He was used to asking questions.

"Husband," she said under her breath.

"Bad split, huh?"

Her mouth tightened. "You could say that."

"You see?" He sat up straight. "That's why I avoid the much-sought-after institution. All my married friends are miserable."

She looked at him, those dark eyes spearing him like a helpless fish. He had the urge to squirm, and he hadn't squirmed in years. "Not all married couples are miserable. Your parents are not the norm. Mine were happily married until my father's death. Mom still misses him and she's never remarried."

Quinn met her glance. "So you still believe in love?"

She gazed off into the distance, not answering for a moment. "Right now I don't trust any man, but I still believe there is such a thing as real, everlasting love. I just chose the wrong man."

"Bargain basement type flashing a Neiman Marcus smile?"

Her mouth curved into a smile and he felt a sucker punch to his heart. "I have no idea what that means, but it fits. He was a phony, a liar, a deceiver, a cheater, a cruel jealous egoistical excuse for a man."

"And the reason you're sensitive about being touched."

Instantly, denial rose in her throat. Answering that question and exposing her weaknesses couldn't happen. Some things were private…and painful. She sat perfectly still, forcing the words down. She wouldn't share intimate details of her life with a stranger. But her ex brought out the worst in her. She just wanted to get out of this place and to her son.

"Wouldn't it be better to start walking?" she asked, to get her mind on something else.

Quinn flung out a hand. "We should head upstream. But rescue teams will be searching along the flooded creek, so we need to stay close."

Two deer emerged from the woods and, startled at the

sight of people, leaped across the meadow. They were so graceful, and Britt watched until she couldn't see them anymore. Silence stretched. Crows landed in a tree, their calls echoing. An armadillo lumbered away into the grass. Animals were leaving their shelters after the storm.

She wiggled her toes, trying to dislodge the caked mud. "How about you—have you ever been married?" It seemed natural to question him, as if they'd been talking all their lives.

"A confirmed happy bachelor."

It was hard to believe that someone as handsome and courageous as Quinn was still available. The good ones were supposed to be taken.

"That's hard to believe."

"The lady has doubts," he mocked with a lifted eyebrow.

"You bet. Trusting men is not my strong suit."

He leaned back on his elbows. "I've had this off-and-on relationship with someone. It suits us both and neither one of us has been eager to tie the knot. I had a date with her last night and she's going to be royally pissed at my no-show."

"I'm sorry." Britt felt responsible.

"Don't be. There have been plenty of times when Deidre hasn't shown up."

Britt frowned. "Sounds as if you don't have much respect for one another."

"Mmm." He sat up. "I'm consumed with my work and she's consumed with spending her father's money. We're aware of each other's faults, but we still get together when the need arises. Bottom line, we're comfortable together."

"That's very candid," Britt said. And routine. And safe. He didn't seem the type of man to choose safe.

"My sister tells me that all the time." He glanced at her, a gleam in his eyes.

That lazy, infectious gaze made her stomach wobble. She cleared her throat. "Are you close to your sister?"

"Yes. I'm five years older and her protector. When she was in her teens I was the one to get her out of trouble before our parents could find out. It became a major job while she was in college. She loved to party and have fun."

"What happened to her?"

"She got arrested."

"What?" That gleam in his eyes intensified. "You're joking."

"Absolutely not. She was arrested for attempting to bribe a sheriff."

"Is she in jail?"

"No. She married the sheriff."

Britt stared at him, not sure whether to believe him or not.

Leaning toward her, Quinn said, "It's true. Peyton was tired of being a party girl, and when she had to look at herself through the sheriff's eyes, she didn't like what she saw. She changed her life. Not for him, but for herself, so she could feel good about her life."

Britt started to speak and he held up a hand, stopping her. "In case you're going to remind me, yes, I know someone who is happily married."

"There's hope for you then."

"Afraid not. I'll be a crusty old bachelor at sixty, yelling at kids who dare to walk on my lawn."

She ran her fingers through the grass. "You don't like kids?"

He shrugged. "I have a niece and a nephew and I'm crazy about them, but I can't see myself as a father."

"Why not?"

The whirl of helicopter blades prevented his answer. Britt jumped to her feet and ran toward the sound. "Here! Please! Stop!" But she only saw the tail of the aircraft as it moved farther south. "No. No. No!" She sank to her knees, frustrated and out of patience.

Quinn stopped beside her. "They must have just picked up someone, or they would have come in this direction."

"We're never going to get out of here."

"We just have to wait." He held out a hand to her. She stared at it for a second and then placed hers in his bigger one. His fingers were strong, capable, and with one tug he pulled her to her feet.

"Thank you," she said, her voice raspy to her own ears.

"That wasn't so hard, was it?" The gleam was back in his eyes, and she sensed he was a man who teased and laughed a lot.

"No," she replied, feeling warm all over. And it wasn't from the sun. After the horrendous night, she felt strong enough to face whatever came next.

Because she'd met a hero.

CARIN DAVIS OPENED THE front door to a deputy sheriff. "Have you found my daughter?" she asked without waiting for an introduction.

"No, ma'am," he answered, removing his hat.

"What's taking so long? It's been hours."

The man took a breath. "The weather's been a hindrance, but they found her car. That's what I came to tell you."

"Oh!" Carin felt the blood drain from her face.

"It was in Brushy Creek." The officer took another breath. "We think the car was swept away into the flooding waters." Carin's knees buckled and the deputy caught her. "Are you okay?"

"Where's…where's my daughter?"

"Rescue teams are out searching, and we've got helicopters. We should know something soon."

But from the young man's voice Carin knew what he was thinking. Britt had drowned in the raging waters.

No!

She refused to believe that.

"Who's at the door?" Ona called.

"A deputy sheriff." Carin stood ramrod straight, not wanting her mother to see her anguish.

Ona hurried to the door, carrying Dillon. He immediately reached for Carin, and she cradled him close. *Mommy will come home, my angel.*

"Where's my granddaughter?" Ona demanded in her usual flame-throwing voice.

"We don't know, ma'am."

"Now listen…"

"They found her car in Brushy Creek, Mama," Carin told her before she could chastise the officer and his department.

"Hail, Mary…" Ona made the sign of the cross and went to the sofa to sit and pray.

"Please let us know the moment you hear anything," Carin said.

"Yes, ma'am. I'm sorry I don't have better news."

"Me, too."

She closed the door and sat by her mother. Ona was the strongest person she knew. She'd lived through the depression, the death of her son and then her husband. Carin never saw fear in her eyes. But she saw it now.

"What are we going to do?" Ona rocked back and forth, her arms wrapped around her ample waist. "Not my Britt… Without her…"

"Don't say it," Carin snapped. She couldn't hear those

words. Britt was her only child, the light of her life, her world. Her young and beautiful daughter had to be alive. Carin couldn't, wouldn't believe anything else.

Sensing the fear in the adults, Dillon began to cry. Loud wails filled the room.

"Shh. Shh, my angel." Carin cuddled him, kissing his fat cheek. "Mommy's coming." He immediately stopped crying, his dark eyes, so like his mother's, opened wide.

"Ma-ma-ma-ma," Dillon chanted, once again happy.

Carin placed him in the Pack 'n Play and gave him a truck to play with.

"You know if that bastard finds out something has happened to Britt he'll be here for the baby."

Carin could process only so much, and didn't want to think about her mother's words. But she had to be prepared.

Ona got to her feet. "I'm looking for Enzo's gun. I'll shoot that bastard before I let him take that child."

"You're not shooting anyone." Carin ran both hands though her short salt-and-pepper hair. "Mama, please, I can't take much more."

"Don't you worry, my pretty." She touched Carin's face. "Mama will take care of everything."

"Mama…" Her cry fell on deaf ears. Ona was already rummaging in her room. Carin sank onto the sofa and buried her face in her hands.

Please, please, bring my baby home, she prayed.

Chapter Three

Britt sat in the wet grass, trying to remain positive, trying not to lose her grip. Quinn lounged beside her, staring at the sky. They both were listening. Waiting.

The sun had chased away the chill and Britt reveled in its warmth. Home. She yearned for home, her baby, mother and grandmother. She couldn't wait to kiss Dillon's fat cheeks, to see his dimples when he smiled. Oh, she missed him. Being away from him for long periods of time was getting harder and harder. But her job paid extremely well and she had benefits. In the lousy economy she couldn't find anything else that would even come close to supporting them.

Of course, Phil paid child support, and he made sure it was always late. Upsetting her was his main objective. He had Dillon every other weekend and a week in the summer, but he never kept to the schedule. She cringed every time he walked out her door with Dillon, but there was nothing she could do to stop him. He had rights, the judge had said. And her drug allegations were unsubstantiated. Being a lawyer, Phil was an expert at fooling people.

Every time he picked up Dillon, the baby cried and clung to her, not wanting to go with a man he rarely saw. Phil always smiled and said, "You know how to stop this. Come back." Those times when Dillon was so upset, she thought about it for a nanosecond, but knew it would be detrimental for her and Dillon. The man had no morals. He couldn't understand why she was so upset. He had told her his drug use and the other women had nothing to do with their marriage.

Britt couldn't believe she'd ever loved the man. Looking back, she saw her first mistake—trusting every word that came out of his mouth. It had been a whirlwind courtship. After two weeks of dating, Phil had asked her to marry him. There wasn't much to think about. He'd wined and dined her until she was head-over-heels for him.

His family was wealthy, his father a senior partner with a lot of clout in a big law firm in Austin. His dad had retired to their home in Colorado, and Phil became a partner in the firm. It was ideal. Britt wouldn't have to work again, Phil had said, but she'd held on to her job, anyway. Now she was glad she had.

Six weeks later they were married, and the fairy tale began. Phil bought her gifts for no reason, hired a maid for the condo and treated Britt as if she were a queen. Then the complaints started. He wanted her to quit her job. He bought sexy clothes, low-cut, short and tight, for her to wear, but she'd refused to look like a hooker. He didn't understand why she had to visit her mother and grandmother so often. At times she wondered if there was anything about her he liked.

On that fatal morning they'd had another argument about her job. When her flight was canceled, she'd decided to quit. Maybe they could get their marriage back on track. She'd just found out she was pregnant, and staying home and being a mother appealed to her.

Hurrying home, she'd stopped for groceries and candles, planning to prepare a special dinner to surprise him. They had been arguing so much she hadn't told him about the baby. But she was the one who'd been surprised. The moment she saw him curled up with the blonde, drug paraphernalia on the nightstand, the fairy tale had ended. Abruptly.

And forever.

He'd begged and pleaded, told her it meant nothing, that it was something he did for stress. She was shocked and sickened at his cavalier attitude. The diseases he had exposed her to were too much to contemplate. She'd walked out there and then, and had never looked back.

After that the threats began. He said she would rue the day she'd left him. Funny, she never had. She just regretted the day she'd met him.

Allowing him access to Dillon was the hardest thing she'd ever had to do. One of his high-priced attorneys made sure it happened. Now she had to deal with Phil for the rest of her life.

She worried about all the bad influences Dillon was exposed to while in Phil's care. That's why she had to make sure this custody attempt was shut down quickly. But for now, she was stuck.

Waiting.

"Do you live with your mother?"

That voice. She was beginning to really like Quinn's smooth, confident voice. The kind that made a woman forget she had morals. Made her forget her distrust of men. And made her forget her dire situation. She'd never met anyone who was so easy to talk to.

"No. I live in Austin. My grandmother lives with my mom, and she's a handful."

"Your grandmother is?" His eyes twinkled.

"She's had a lot of sadness in her life and it's hardened her. She doesn't take crap from anyone."

"So she's an angry old woman?" He ran a hand around the collar of his shirt to loosen the drying mud.

"She's hard-nosed about a lot of things. It's not easy to explain." Britt gazed into the distance. "One October her neighbors made a Halloween scene on their lawn with hay, pumpkins and ghosts. My grandmother said part of it was on her property, and she asked them to remove it. They didn't, so she set fire to it."

He laughed. "You're kidding."

"No." Britt shook her head. "The neighbors called the cops and they contacted my mother. To keep my grand-mother out of jail, my mom paid for the damages, but never told Onnie. That's what I call my grandmother."

"Does she do things like that often?"

"Yes, and it's very frustrating for my mom. The last episode was the straw that broke the camel's back, so to speak. Onnie always has a big garden in her backyard, and she does a lot of canning. Two years ago she said her neighbor, not the same one, was stealing her tomatoes. My mom told her she just forgets she's picked them, but Onnie wouldn't believe that for a second."

"What did she do?"

Britt didn't miss the laughter in Quinn's voice. That was not the usual effect Onnie had on people.

Britt shifted into a more comfortable position. "Her uncle Enzo is ninety-two, and he gave her an old World War II pistol for protection after my grandfather died. I'm not sure it even has bullets, but Onnie took it over to the neighbors and told them if she caught them in her garden she was going to shoot them. Of course, they called the police about the crazy lady with a gun. My mom thought it was time for Onnie to move, since she wasn't welcome in the neighborhood anymore."

"So she moved in with your mother?"

"Yes, and it hasn't been easy. Onnie is stubborn, but they're managing to get along. At least Mom is keeping her out of trouble."

The drying mud was becoming uncomfortable. Britt shifted again to ease the tightness of her jeans. "These pants are drying like paint, and I'm never going to be able to remove them."

"Call me and I'll come help you."

She glanced at him, expecting laughter on his face, but there wasn't any. "I never know when you're teasing."

His eyes held hers. "I'm not teasing."

Tiny pinpoints of heat dotted her body, and she was sure her clothes were melting off under his warm gaze. In his eyes she saw the one thing she'd been avoiding for a very long time—desire. She was surprised she could still recognize it. But she was about to drown in pure, pure waves of blue.

His hand gently moved tangles of hair from her face. Everything faded away. They were two people, a man and a woman, stranded in the woods and discovering a whole new realm of emotions. And Britt wasn't uncomfortable with the discovery.

"I'm not sensitive about being touched," she blurted out.

He lifted an eyebrow. "Really? It seemed that way to me."

She glanced down at her hands and saw the dirt and grime. "Since you saved my life, I have to be honest with you." She wiped her palms down her jeans. "I haven't been with anyone since my marriage ended." She hadn't meant to get this personal, but she couldn't seem to stop herself. "When you touched me, I was feeling emotions I hadn't felt in a long time, and it made me angry. I was fighting for my life and you're a stranger. I shouldn't feel attracted to you."

"Are you thinking your senses were just heightened?"

She raised her head to look at him. "Has to be."

"Want to put it to the test?" His voice was seductive, lulling her into a relaxed state. There was only one answer in her head. Yes!

He lifted the heavy hair from her neck and she had no qualms about meeting his kiss. Her heart hammered in expectation and...

They both heard it.

The helicopter.

Britt jumped up, running with her arms in the air. "Here! Here! We're here!"

She tripped and fell headlong in the grass. Quinn fell down beside her, laughing. "You fall more than any woman I know."

"I do not," she stated, laughter bubbling inside her. She sat up and without thinking hugged and kissed him lightly. "Thank you."

"Britt..."

The loud sound of the copter drowned out his words. In less than a minute the aircraft landed. Two men jumped out.

"Are you okay?" one called.

"Yes," Quinn shouted back, helping Britt to her feet.

They were assisted aboard, then were headed for Austin. After a paramedic checked her vitals, Britt asked, "May I please call my mother?"

"Yes, ma'am."

She talked for a moment, just to let her mom know she was fine. She also told her where the aircraft was taking her. It wasn't long before they landed at Breckenridge Hospital in Austin.

These were Britt's last moments with Quinn. Why she was feeling nostalgic she wasn't sure. She looked up to find him staring at her.

"I hope you find that real love. Don't settle for anything less," he murmured.

She swallowed and wondered if there was such a thing as finding love with a stranger. Pushing the thought aside, she said, "Good luck with Deidre. I hope she's not too upset with you."

He leaned over and kissed her forehead. "Goodbye, Britt."

"Goodbye," she whispered with a lump in her throat.

Stretchers were rolled out to the helicopter, and Britt and Quinn were whisked away for a thorough examination.

She got a glimpse of the sky and saw it was darkening once again. They'd been rescued just in time. Turning her head, she noticed Quinn being pushed into an E.R. room down the hall. A pretty blonde ran to hug him. A man in khakis, a white shirt and boots, with a badge on his chest, followed. It had to be Quinn's sister and the sheriff. Quinn had his family. Britt was happy about that.

Together for less than twenty-four hours, and now they'd be separated for a lifetime.

Goodbye, Quinn.

My hero.

"Britt, my baby." Carin rushed into the E.R. room, cradling Dillon on her hip. Onnie was right behind them. It was the most beautiful sight Britt had ever seen.

Carin took a startled look at her, no doubt surprised at how bedraggled she was, and hugged her. "Are you okay?"

"I'm fine now."

Dillon wiggled from his grandmother to his mother.

"No…" Carin started, but Britt grabbed her baby and held him.

She soaked up his sweet scent, kissing his cheek. His heart beat rapidly against her. "Ma-ma-ma," he cooed.

A nurse came in. "Everyone will have to leave. I have to check the patient and get her cleaned up."

"Now listen here, missy." Onnie stepped up to the plate, fire in her eyes. "This is my granddaughter and I ain't leaving her."

"Mama," Carin said in a sharp voice that usually got Onnie's attention. "We'll go to the waiting room until they've checked Britt. We need to know she's okay."

"How long is it going to take?" The question was directed at the nurse.

"Not long. I'll come and get you when the doctor has completed his exam."

"Yeah. Like I believe that." Onnie snorted. "I wasn't born yesterday, missy."

"Onnie, please," Britt begged, nuzzling Dillon.

Her grandmother patted her hand. "I'll be just down the hall. If you need anything, just holler. I still got good ears." Onnie looked her over. "My, you're a mess. Looks like someone used you as a mop."

Carin reached for Dillon. He clung to Britt. "It's okay, sweetie. Mommy's right here. Go with Nana."

Reluctantly, he let go, his bottom lip trembling. Britt felt herself wobble as they walked out. "Please hurry," she told the nurse. She wanted to hold her son until her arms couldn't hold him any longer.

Within minutes the nurse had cut off Britt's clothes, and a doctor came in to examine her. She had scratches and bruises, but he wanted some tests run, mostly a Cat scan of her head and an X-ray of her lungs.

She begged for a shower first and the doctor allowed it.

The nurse took her down the hall to a bathroom and stayed with her just in case she passed out. Britt scrubbed her hair twice before she'd removed all the mud and grime. Quinn was right—soap and water did the trick. Stepping out, she wondered if he was also taking a shower.

She had to stop thinking about him.

A few minutes later she was back in her room. The nurse said they'd take her for tests soon. Britt felt one hundred percent better. Almost. The custody hearing was still hanging over her head. What was Phil up to? Caring for their son wasn't on his list of priorities.

Her mother slipped into the room.

"Mom. Where's Dillon?" Britt sat up.

Carin tucked her hair behind her ears in a nervous gesture. "Don't worry. He's with Onnie. I just wanted to make sure you were okay."

"I'm fine." A tear trailed from her eye, belying her words.

Her mother gathered her into her arms. "Oh, my baby, I've been so worried."

Britt clutched her. "I was so stupid going out in the storm, but I had to see my son."

Carin sat down on the bed. "What happened?"

"It was awful." Britt scrubbed at her eyes, telling her mother the whole story.

"What a courageous young man," Carin said.

"I couldn't have held on to the log much longer, Mom. I…"

"Shh, my baby." Carin wiped away Britt's tears. "You're alive and we have to thank this man."

"I have…several times." Britt sat up straighter. "Have you seen any reporters in the hospital?"

"There was one talking to a nurse, trying to get information, but she said she couldn't help him."

"Good. I don't want any of this to get back to Phil."

Carin frowned. "I'm sure it will be on the news."

"Not if we don't give them any information." Britt tugged at her hospital gown. "Would you mind going to my apartment and getting me a change of clothes? By then I should be through with the tests and able to leave."

"You got it." Her mother kissed her forehead. "Try not to worry. There's no way Phil can take Dillon."

Britt sincerely hoped that was true.

For the next hour she underwent tests, but they didn't find anything and the doctor finally released her, telling her to check with her own doctor if she had any problems. Her mother came back with her clothes and Britt quickly dressed. Determined to avoid reporters, she told her mother to pull the car to the front entrance instead of the E.R. That way she could dodge the press. The last thing she wanted was having her picture in the papers.

"Here's your wheelchair," the nurse said.

"No, that's fine."

The woman scowled. "I'm sorry. It's policy and—"

"I really can walk. I don't want to face any newspeople and I don't want any media attention."

Something in her voice must have gotten to the nurse. She chewed on her lip. "I'll take you out a back way." She held up a finger. "But in a wheelchair."

Britt nodded, grateful for her help.

The ride was short. The nurse stopped at a door. "This will take you to the front entrance."

"Thank you. I appreciate it."

"Just stay out of rising waters," the woman replied with a smile.

Britt nodded and opened the door. She stopped as she saw a group down the hall. Quinn was dressed in dark slacks and a white shirt, and a different tall blonde was hugging him. Had to be Deidre. Evidently she'd forgiven him. Quinn's sister and her sheriff stood to the side.

Britt's eyes were glued to Quinn's tall lean frame. Her heart pounded against her ribs as she said another silent goodbye to the man who had risked his life to save hers.

Why were the good ones always taken?

Chapter Four

During the next couple of days Britt spent a lot of time filling out papers for her insurance company, getting a new driver's license and reporting lost credit cards. The company rented her a car until all the paperwork was finalized and approved.

Every morning she seemed to find a new ache or pain. Her body had taken a beating in the water, but each day she felt better and stronger. Strong enough to face Phil in court.

She met with her lawyer, Mona Tibbs, and Mona assured her they had nothing to worry about. It was just another attempt of Phil's to scare her into returning to him. After talking to Mona, Britt felt optimistic. Returning to Phil wasn't an option.

All through the busyness and worry, Britt thought often of Quinn. He lived in Austin, but she didn't even know his last name. She'd like to send him a thank-you, a gift of some sort. And she had to admit she'd like to see him again. Maybe Phil hadn't destroyed all her trust in men.

The temperature hovered in the forties on the day of the hearing. Her mother was coming into Austin to sit with Dillon while Britt was at the hearing. When her doorbell rang, Britt knew who it was, so she ran to let her mother in. She was surprised to see her grandmother, too.

"I've decided to go with you," her mother informed her. "Mama will stay with Dillon."

"There's no need." Britt tried to reassure her. "Mona says it will take only a few minutes. Phil doesn't have a leg to stand on. A judge hardly ever takes a child away from a loving mother."

"Still, I'd feel better if you weren't alone."

"Mom..." Britt didn't get to voice her complaint as Onnie pushed passed her to the small kitchenette.

"Do you have any beer?" her grandmother asked, opening the refrigerator.

"What? Beer?" Britt's thoughts zipped in a completely different direction.

"Mama, you're not drinking beer this early in the day," Carin snapped.

"It's not for me. It's for Enzo." Onnie stopped snooping in the refrigerator and faced her daughter.

"Enzo!" Carin's voice rose a notch.

Britt closed the front door with a sigh. She didn't need this today.

"Yeah. His assisted living facility is not far away. I told him he can catch the bus and come visit."

"No, no." Carin shook her head. "Not today."

Onnie placed her hands on her hips. "You may be my daughter but you can't boss me around."

"Please, could we not argue?" Britt asked. "I'm nervous enough."

Onnie hugged her. "Don't worry. That sleazebag is not taking sweet Dillon." She shot a glance at her daughter. "But we're visiting Enzo before we go home."

"Fine," Carin replied through tight lips.

Britt picked up her purse. "I really have to run. The hearing is at two."

"I'm ready," her mother said, and Britt knew there was no way to dissuade her.

She turned to her grandmother. "Dillon is down for his nap. When he wakes up..."

"I know the drill, my pretty." Onnie pinched her cheek and reached for the TV remote control. "We'll be just dandy. Go stick it to the bastard."

THE RIDE TO FAMILY COURT was done mostly in silence. Britt was nervous and she couldn't shake it. Mona met them outside the courtroom. In her forties, with a blond bob, the lawyer was impeccably dressed in a dark suit and heels. Britt liked her confident attitude.

"This shouldn't take long," Mona said. "Your ex has to show just cause to remove Dillon from your care, and he simply doesn't have any grounds." She touched Britt's forearm. "Relax."

"I'm trying to," she replied, feeling her face muscles stretch into tight lines of worry. But she knew Phil well enough to know he was up to something. She wouldn't relax until this was over.

Footsteps echoed on the tiled floor. Britt looked up to see Phil strolling toward her, a tall man blocked by Phil's frame behind him. Blond and green-eyed, Phil was suave, handsome, a man who had once turned her head with his charm and words of love. His attraction and phony words had been exposed for what they really were, and now he just turned her stomach.

"Good afternoon, Roslyn," he said in a voice that slid across her nerves with the sharpness of a nail. He always called her by her first name. At first it had been charming. Now it was insulting.

"There is nothing good about any meeting with you," she managed to say.

"Tut-tut. You need to keep that temper in check."

Temper? What was he talking about?

"Phil, I don't think…"

That voice! It resonated in Britt's head with sweet memories as she gaped at the man who stepped forward. *No. It couldn't be.*

But it was.

Her hero from the creek stood staring at her with the same look of shock she was sure was on her face.

"Roslyn, this is my lawyer, Quentin Ross."

Quentin Ross.

In the stunned silence no one spoke. The sturdy, efficient clock on the wall ticked away seconds like a time bomb. Voices echoed down the hall. A faint scent of aftershave filled her nostrils. Behind Britt a door opened, the turning of the door handle sounding like cymbals in her ears.

"The judge will see you now," a lady said.

Mona nudged her. "Let's go inside."

"Are you okay?" her mother asked. "You're as white as a sheet."

"I'm fine," she muttered, but somewhere deep inside her she knew she was never going to be the same again.

They took seats on the right of the judge's desk. Britt was glad of the chair for support. Her legs were trembling. She drew a long breath, forcing herself to breathe in and out in a normal rhythm. But there was nothing normal about the fear gripping her throat.

He was Phil's lawyer kept running through her mind like a 9-1-1 call. Her hero, the man she'd put on a pedestal, was now supporting Phil to take Dillon from her. How could that be? He had to know Phil in some way. What had she revealed to him in the woods? Had she inadvertently hurt her case?

She was searching for answers, but didn't find any.

Gripping her hands together until they were bloodless, she looked around the room. The Texan and American flags hung in one corner. Polished dark wood and brass were all around her. Dark and forbidding—much like the feeling in her heart. She shivered.

It took a full minute for her shock to dissipate and her strength to kick in. She didn't care who Phil's attorney was. Quentin Ross didn't matter. Keeping her son did. She focused on that, but had to resist looking Quinn's way. She couldn't believe how hard that was.

The judge entered from a side door and took her seat at the big desk. "Good afternoon," she said, folding her hands on the file folders in front of her. "I'm Judge Evelyn Norcutt and we're here today at the request of Phil Rutherford to modify custody of minor child Dillon Allan Rutherford." She fingered a piece of paper on the desk. "I received this memo yesterday. Ms. Tibbs, I assume you've received it, too."

"Yes, Your Honor."

"Do you have any objections?"

"No, Your Honor."

"What is it?" Britt whispered.

"Mr. Rutherford's original attorney is ill and Mr. Ross is taking over."

"Why didn't you tell me this?" she hissed.

"I didn't think it mattered."

"It matters when—"

"Mr. Ross!" The judge's strong voice broke through her words. "You're taking a step down by visiting us in family court."

Quinn stood, and against her will Britt looked at him. In a dark blue suit, white shirt and a blue-striped tie he looked all-business. No mud, no grime, no mischievous grin, just business behind a brooding expression. She noticed his hair was a medium blond streaked with an even lighter shade. Her guess would be that he spent a lot of time in the sun.

With Deidre.

Britt gritted her teeth. Quinn Ross meant nothing to her.

"Your Honor, I'm helping out a friend. I spent a year in family law before switching to defense. I'm more than qualified to handle this case."

His deep, confident voice sliced through her as memories of lightning and thunder rumbled in her head.

"I have no doubt."

Friend. She picked up on that one word. He was friends with Phil. She'd been married to Phil for six months and she'd never heard of him.

The judge pushed her glasses up the bridge of her nose. "I've gone over the petition Mr. Wallis filed with the court." She glanced over the top of her glasses at Quinn. "I assume you're up-to-date."

"Yes, Your Honor. I spoke with Herb over the phone about every detail of the case."

"Good." The judge opened a folder and pulled out papers. "Seems Mr. Rutherford is concerned about the amount of time Ms. Rutherford—"

"It's Davis," Britt corrected, before she could stop herself. "I took back my maiden name."

The judge looked up with a frown. "Davis, then. Mr. Rutherford is concerned about the amount of time Ms. Davis spends away from their son."

"Your Honor." Mona was on her feet. "I've seen the petition and it's completely misleading, a blatant attempt to discredit Ms. Davis's abilities as a mother. Ms. Davis is an international flight attendant. It requires her to be gone for long periods."

"I'm aware of that, and I'm also aware she has a nine-month-old son."

"Ms. Davis's mother takes very good care of him while Ms. Davis is away."

"But Dillon is not being cared for by either of his parents." The judge flipped through the papers. "A six-month work log of Ms. Davis has also been filed by Mr. Wallis. In June and July she was home only one week each month. That concerns me."

"Your Honor." Britt had to speak. She could feel this spiraling in the wrong direction. "I took the summer flights to make extra money to support my child. It's not something I do on a regular basis. And when I'm away, I speak with him every morning, and every night before he goes to bed. I love my son and I'm trying to make a better life for him."

"But you're not there for him physically."

The truth of that hit her in the chest like a sledgehammer, and she had no words to defend herself.

"Mr. Ross." The judge turned her attention to Quinn. "Do you have anything to add?"

"Yes, Your Honor." He stood and buttoned his jacket. "With Ms. Davis's...busy schedule, Mr. Rutherford is concerned about his son being raised...by a grandmother. He's offering...to be there for the boy full time...morning, night and he'll come home for lunch. Mr. Rutherford will hire a nanny for when he's at work. I submit...that at this time Philip Rutherford...is the better parent to raise Dillon Allan."

The judge frowned. "Mr. Ross, is there something wrong with your voice?"

Quinn raised a hand to his neck. "I have a bit of a sore throat."

"Thought so. Your usual stellar voice is a little off, but nonetheless effective."

"Do something," Britt whispered to Mona. "Don't let them take my son." The fear in her became very real. She felt it with every beat of her heart. Phil's father was very powerful in Austin, and somehow they had gotten to the judge. That was the only explanation. And they'd hired Quentin Ross to deliver the blow that would rip out Britt's heart.

Mona was on her feet once again. "Your Honor, they're using Ms. Davis's job as a weapon to take her son. A baby needs to be with his mother."

The judge folded her hands on the papers. "I agree, Ms. Tibbs, a baby needs to be with his mother. But Ms. Davis isn't there. She's a drop-in mother. A nine-month-old boy needs more. He needs a full-time mother. A full-time parent."

"A lot of mothers work."

"But they're there in the morning and at night. As the situation stands I see no recourse but—"

"No." Britt jumped to her feet. "You can't take my son. He's my life. I'm his *mother*."

"Ms. Davis, I rarely take a child from the mother, but as I said, and Mr. Rutherford's lawyer has stated, you're not there for your baby. Until your situation changes I'm granting temporary custody to the father, Phil Rutherford."

"No, no, don't do this. Can't you see what they're doing? Don't, please." Tears rolled from her eyes and she quickly brushed them away. She felt her mother's arm around her waist and she leaned on her for support.

"I said temporary, Ms. Davis. I'll review this case in four months. That will give you time to sort out your life." She turned to the laptop on her left and typed in information.

"You are to hand over the boy to Mr. Rutherford at ten in the morning and—"

"No," Britt said with force. "I refuse to hand over my child to a drug addict. You're endangering his life. What kind of judge are you?"

"Sit down, Ms. Davis."

Britt stared at the judge, anger in every bone of her body. If the judge thought she would back down, she was in for a shock. Britt had nothing left to lose. "Isn't this supposed to be about the best interest of the child? Well, you've just blown that to hell with your bigoted attitude."

"Ms. Tibbs, get your client under control or I will hold her in contempt."

"Let me handle this, Britt," Mona whispered. "You don't need to go to jail. Sit down, please."

Her mother tugged her back into her chair.

"Thank you," the judge said. "As I was saying, all child support will stop. Sundays, from eight in the morning until five in the afternoon, will be Ms. Davis's time to see Dillon, and every Tuesday and Thursday afternoon from one to six, if her schedule permits. Mr. Rutherford, I expressly do not want you there during those times, and order no contact between you and Ms. Davis. Mr. Ross's office will oversee the visits."

"My client will not be allowed any time alone with her child?" Mona asked rather tartly.

"With her connection to the airlines, she's a flight risk. For now, someone will always be with her."

Britt gritted her teeth at the injustice.

"I object to this, Your Honor. Ms. Davis is a loving mother and I resent you using her job as a means to remove her child from her. I resent it as a woman and as a lawyer."

"Resent away. You have that right."

"I'll file an appeal."

"Go ahead, but my ruling stands. This court is adjourned."

Just like that they had taken her child. Her precious baby.

Britt was numb and empty and couldn't focus on what to do next. There *was* no next. Phil would raise Dillon for the next four months. He'd won.

They had taken her child. It was her worst nightmare come true.

Her mother hugged her. "Baby, I'm so sorry, but we'll get through this."

"I don't know how," she murmured, looking down at her broken nails from her time in the creek. A choked sob left her throat and she raised her head. Her eyes collided with Quinn's. His blue eyes were somber, almost apologetic. She immediately looked away and grabbed her coat. She would not let him see her cry.

Picking up her purse, she walked from the room, her mother beside her.

Phil waited at the door, a smirk on his face. "I'll be at your apartment at ten in the morning for Dillon."

She couldn't speak; pain and anger locked her vocal cords. Without a word, she pushed by him. He grabbed her arm and she jerked away.

"Don't touch me."

"Leave my daughter alone," Carin said. "Haven't you hurt her enough?"

Ignoring her mother, Phil looked straight at Britt. "You know how to stop this."

Yes, she did, but she'd rather die first. And that's what she was doing, dying inside. She walked away without giving him any satisfaction.

And she refused to even spare Quentin Ross a glance.

QUINN WATCHED THIS EXCHANGE with a knot in his gut. He felt as if he had been sucker punched by the heavyweight champion of the world. Or maybe by a devious, cunning, so-called friend.

"What did you mean by that?"

Instead of answering, Phil slapped Quinn on the back. "You did great today, old friend."

He wasn't Phil's friend. They'd been classmates in law school. Through that connection, Quinn had gotten an internship in Philip Sr.'s prestigious law firm. He was deeply grateful, but he didn't want to continue to pay that debt for the rest of his life.

Quinn placed papers in his briefcase and snapped it shut. "Why did you call me to handle this case at the last minute?"

"Because you're the best. And since Herb was indisposed, I knew you were the one who could stick it to Roslyn in a big way. Dad's going to be so excited to hear Dillon will be living with me."

"I didn't accept as a favor to your father." Who was he kidding? It was the only reason. Quinn's law career was his life, and Philip Sr. could ruin it with just a couple of calls. It wasn't easy admitting that, and Quinn felt lower than the dust lingering beneath the rug on the floor. "I did it because I thought your ex was a lousy mother and a tramp, like you and Herb painted her."

Phil punched him on the arm as if they were teenagers. "She got to you with that sweet demeanor and gorgeous looks, not to mention totally awesome body."

Phil didn't know the half of it. "I don't like taking a child from his mother."

"Don't worry, she'll be back in my bed by the end of the week."

Quinn frowned. "Is that what this hearing was about?"

"You bet. I know how to push her buttons, and now she knows I have the upper hand."

Quinn picked up his briefcase. "Don't call me for any more help. My specialty is defense law and that's where I'm staying."

"Now, ol' buddy, Herb is out of commission, so you're the lawyer of record for this case. You wouldn't want me to tell Dad that you bailed."

Quinn kept a tight rein on his temper. "You really are a jerk."

Phil's face darkened. "Don't push your luck."

"I'm only just starting." He walked away without another word, but he left his dignity, his ethics and his self-respect behind.

What had he done?

Chapter Five

Quinn sat in his paneled study surrounded by bookshelves holding his father's ancient-history tomes. Taking a sip of wine, he gazed at the leather-bound relics neatly lined up on the shelves. Books were also haphazardly stacked on the hardwood floor. He'd been meaning to donate some to a library, but so far hadn't gotten round to it. Sometime soon he needed to call Professor Withers, a colleague of his dad's, and offer him some volumes.

Peyton had taken the ones she'd wanted, but the room was still full of the books his father loved. As a history professor, Malcolm Ross's focus was the past. Though he'd been a quiet, gentle man, his voice would rise in excitement as he spoke of ancient civilizations. Egypt, Greece and China were his favorite places, and in the summers Quinn and Peyton would travel with their father to explore the fascinating ruins of those countries.

Quinn never found an interest in the past. He was more like his mother, who was also a lawyer. But he respected his father more than anyone he'd ever known. The man never complained or judged.

Quinn poured another glass of wine, wishing he could talk to his dad, who had a way of solving problems with logic and reason.

And Quinn had one big problem.

Britt.

She was Phil's ex.

Quinn was supposed to be smart, but he couldn't wrap his brain around that. Rarely was his composure shaken. He'd mastered the appearance of calm over the years in the courtroom. But today, when he saw Britt and realized she was Phil's ex, he'd almost lost his grip on himself.

The woman he'd saved in the creek was Phil's ex-wife. Phil had cheated, lied and deceived her, and he was the reason she had an aversion to being touched. Quinn believed everything Britt had told him. She had no reason to lie. And Quinn had stood in open court and followed the plan Phil and Herb had laid out to take her child. Because he owed Philip Sr.

The thought left a bitter taste in his mouth.

He took a gulp of wine. He'd been planning to call her to see how she was, but his busy schedule had prevented him from following through. Now she would probably never speak to him again. He didn't blame her.

He yanked off his tie and took his wine to the large living area with the floor-to-ceiling windows overlooking the pool. Since it was winter, the pool was covered, but he rarely used it, anyway. He sank onto the sofa and propped his feet on the hundred-year-old coffee table that had belonged to his ancestors on his father's side. He took another big swallow of wine. His father had been raised in the colonial revival style house, as had Peyton and Quinn. Quinn had bought out Peyton's share, and now the sprawling house was his—one man and more rooms than he'd ever use. The quiet of those empty rooms seemed to gnaw at him, reminding him he was alone.

And he'd never felt lonelier.

He stared at a family photo on the limestone fireplace. The four people in it were smiling and looked happy. In retrospect, Quinn knew they hadn't been. His mother had found happiness with other men. His father had buried himself in the past. When Quinn was older he'd spent a lot of time away from home, and Peyton had rebelled in every way she could. Not a happy family, but they'd survived, because despite all that they still loved each other.

He ran his hands through his hair, knowing he was avoiding what was really bothering him.

Britt.

He'd thought she was beautiful, all bedraggled in the creek, but today she'd eclipsed that. She'd been eye-catching in a silky print dress that hugged her curvy body. Her dark hair had hung loose around her shoulders, making her eyes look that much darker. Her skin had glowed and her eyes had sparkled—until she'd spotted him. Then it was like someone turned off a light. That expression on her face had cut right through him.

What had he done?

He prided himself on the one thing he did well—being a lawyer. For the first time he felt tainted by his profession. He placed his empty glass on the table.

Something wasn't quite right with what had happened today. The last-minute call. The documents all being filed. Did Phil know Quinn had a connection to Britt? Quinn hadn't given out any interviews, and he hadn't seen anything about the incident in the paper. But he felt as if every detail had been staged—for Britt's benefit—to humiliate her.

He hurried toward his study, retrieved his cell phone and punched in Herb's number.

"Herb, it's Quinn," he said as the lawyer clicked on.

"Thanks for filling in today. I heard it went well."

"From who?"

There was a long pause. "Phil, of course."

"All the damaging info on Roslyn Davis was just a little too convenient. Luckily, I didn't have to use it." Britt's many affairs were listed in a file with the men's names and dates. Her vicious, jealous temper was documented, along with dates of when she had trashed Phil's condo. Photos were attached in a folder, but Quinn hadn't had a chance to look at them. Now he wished he had taken the time.

"Are you questioning my research and my investigators?" Herb's voice grew angry.

So did Quinn's. "You're goddamn right I am."

Another long pause. "Stay out of it, Quinn."

"I'd love to do that, Herb, but for some reason I've been cast smack-dab in the middle."

"If you value your law career, you'll leave it alone."

That was the crux of the whole situation. Everyone knew what his law career meant to him, especially Phil and Philip Sr.

"A mother lost her child today. I can't leave that alone."

"Everything will work out."

You know how to stop this. Phil's words came back to him, and Quinn wondered how long it would be before Britt caved to her ex's demands. How long could she live without her child? Phil gave her a week, but Quinn knew she was much stronger than that.

"To whose advantage?"

"I can't answer that. I just did my job."

"Or what you were told to do. That folder on Roslyn Davis was very inflammatory, and I suspect very little of it was true. And it's strange that you don't sound the least bit sick now, not like yesterday, when you were wheezing to catch a breath."

"This conversation is over."

"You're damn right it is." Quinn slammed his phone onto the desk.

He paced in his study. His first instinct was to resign from the case, but then sleazy attorneys willing to do anything for money would take over, and Britt's fate would be sealed.

Philip would blackball him and no one would win except the Rutherfords. Quinn had to stick this out one way or another.

THAT NIGHT IN HIS BEDROOM he went through the folder of photos that Herb had sent him. There were several pictures of Britt with pilots and businessmen, and dates and names were written on the back. None of the photos showed any signs of intimacy between Britt and the men, but they were damaging because it looked as if she was partying while away from her son. Evidently, Phil had her watched all the time.

Watched!

Was the detective tailing her the night of the storm? Had he seen them being rescued? Was that the reason Phil had called him to handle the case—to make Britt aware that Phil knew her every move? If so, the man was a sick son of a bitch.

There were photos that showed his trashed condo. Apparently, she'd lost control of her temper more than once. Even though he could see the photos, something about them didn't ring true. He'd spent twenty-four hours with the woman and he knew beyond a shadow of a doubt that this was not the real Roslyn Britt Davis.

How he wished he had looked at these photos earlier. If he had, he would never have stepped foot in that courtroom. *Right?* He fervently believed he wouldn't have, but the truth taunted his conscience.

Would he jeopardize everything he'd worked for over the years? Would he tarnish his law career?

He put the folder back in his briefcase, took a shower and went to bed. Closing his eyes, he recalled her face when she'd spotted him in the courtroom. Her expression had held blatant fear. It wasn't the same fear he'd seen in her at the creek. This was basic, primal, and it reinforced the horror that she'd just lost everything she loved. Then anger had quickly replaced the fear.

And it had been directed at him.

Turning over, he groaned. After rescuing her from the creek, he somehow knew their lives would irrevocably be woven together. Thrown together by tragedy and bound by its aftereffects.

But not like this.

She now hated him.

The thought lingered in his mind as he fell asleep.

BRITT SLEPT WITH DILLON in her arms. She knew it wasn't good for him, but she couldn't help herself. She had to hold him, to feel him. The darkness of the night closed around them, keeping them together for now. His soft breathing tickled her chin, and she held on because it would be a long time before she'd hold him like this again.

She wanted to explain to him what would happen tomorrow, but he wouldn't understand. She didn't understand herself. How could the judge give custody to Phil? How could her job be a factor? How could Quinn be involved in this?

The questions kept beating at her and the answers continued to elude her. She forced herself not to think about Quinn. He'd saved her life, and she'd always be grateful for that. But he'd saved it just to take it. She pushed the thought away because it only upset her more.

Her mother had wanted to spend the night, but Britt insisted she go home. Now Britt desperately wanted someone to talk to.

She closed her eyes, but didn't sleep. The pain was too deep for any rest. At six she got up and carried Dillon to his crib. The apartment had only one bedroom, so they shared the space. When she had enough money saved, she was going to look for a bigger place. That's why she'd taken the extra flights this summer—for the money. She'd never dreamed her decision would come back to haunt her.

Gently, she laid Dillon down and covered him, staring at his precious face. The night-light was just bright enough for her to see his chubby cheeks and dark hair. A choked sob left her throat and she tore herself away from him to go take a shower. In fifteen minutes she was dressed for this horrible day.

All during the night thoughts of running had plagued her. She could be out of the country in no time, but she knew deep down that being on the run was no life for Dillon or her. She would stay and fight.

There was only one way to do that—to make a secure, happy home for Dillon with his mother there at all times. Somewhere during the night Britt realized she had to quit her job. Being with the airlines eight years, she'd built up seniority. But that security meant nothing without her son. Once that decision was made she felt better.

Phil would not keep her son.

She pulled a suitcase from the closet and began to pack Dillon's clothes. Then she made lists: of Dillon's schedule, his nap times, medication for his sniffles or colds, foods she was now feeding him, what he liked at bedtime and so on. The list was for the nanny; Phil would have little to do with his son.

She gave Phil lists all the time when he picked up Dillon,

but she suspected he just threw them away. This time she tucked them in with Dillon's clothes, so the nanny would find the lists and use them.

As she packed Dillon's toys, she vowed she wouldn't cry. This was only temporary, but it didn't keep that crippling pain at bay. She would be strong—and it would take every ounce of courage she had.

After the suitcase was packed, she carried it to the front door. She couldn't bear a long goodbye. Back in the bedroom, she brushed her hair and clipped it back. As she did, she heard, "Ma-ma-i-ah-o-ma."

Dillon's chatter warmed her cold heart. He stood holding on to the rail of his crib. The first time he'd done that it had shocked her. He was too young to stand, but she had a feeling her son was going to do everything early. He moved his feet as if he were standing in hot ashes. He crawled the same way—fast. Soon he would be walking everywhere. Oh, she hoped she didn't miss that. She swallowed, telling herself not to cry.

She changed his diaper and dressed him. As she slipped a long-sleeved T-shirt over his head, he started to whine. He wanted his bottle. She knew that sound.

"Just a minute, precious." She kissed his cheek and carried him to the kitchen, placing him in his high chair. He slapped his hands on the tray while she prepared his milk. When he saw the bottle, he bounced up and down and grabbed for it eagerly. She had a hard time getting his bib on.

After she fed him his cereal and part of a banana, she washed his face and again changed his diaper. She wanted Dillon clean when Phil took him.

She sat with him on the sofa. His big brown eyes stared at her.

"Mommy loves you."

"Ma-oh-ah-ma-ma," he cooed, his two new bottom teeth gleaming.

How did she tell him?

"You'll be staying with Daddy for a while." Her throat closed up. She had to swallow. "Mommy will see you on Sunday. I love you, love you, love you, my Dilly bear."

"Ma-ma-ma-ma." He bounced in her arms.

"Give me a kiss."

He placed his wet mouth against her cheek and she held him as tightly as she could. Maybe too tight, for he wiggled to get free. It was play time and he wanted down. Just as she was about to place him on the floor, the doorbell rang. Her heart rate skyrocketed into overdrive.

She glanced at the clock on the oven and saw it was exactly ten—time to have the courage to let go. She gritted her teeth, wishing she could hold back the seconds. The inevitable. Cradling Dillon close, she walked to the door. The only thing that gave her the strength to do so was that she knew Phil would not hurt his own son. He might be uncaring and unfeeling, but he would pay someone to look after Dillon. That was the irony of the whole ordeal. Phil didn't want Dillon. He just wanted Britt's attention and eventual surrender.

Never.

Breathing in the sweet scent of her baby, she felt a stub of temptation. But only for a second.

She took a deep breath and opened the door. Phil stood there with his usual smirk, the nanny, who she had met before, behind him. Quinn stood to the side, briefcase in hand. She ignored him.

"Is the boy ready?" Phil asked.

"Yes," she murmured, keeping her features set in a mask of pain.

As soon as Dillon saw Phil, he buried his face in her neck and clung to her like he always did. And that made it so hard. She rubbed his back, trying to soothe him.

"His clothes are packed," she said, glancing at the case at her feet.

"No lists?" Phil asked with a lifted brow.

"Would it do any good?"

"Let's go," Quinn intervened. "The judge advises as little contact as possible." He just wanted to get the transfer over with, and he could see that Phil wanted to linger, to keep needling Britt.

Phil shot him a cold stare, but Quinn didn't back down.

"Get the case." Phil spoke to the nanny and reached for his son. The boy tried to wiggle as far away as possible. Britt's features tightened in pain and Quinn felt a jolt in his heart. How had he gotten involved in this?

Phil gripped the boy around his waist and tried to pull him away from Britt. In doing so he made sure his hands touched her breasts. A look of disgust spread over her face, a look she couldn't disguise.

As Phil pulled Dillon away, the boy began to cry loudly, hands outstretched toward his mother. Britt clasped trembling hands to her face, and Quinn had to look away. *This is wrong,* he kept thinking, but there was nothing he could do. For now.

"You know how to stop this," Phil said to Britt, and the sadness in her eyes turned to anger. In that instance, Quinn knew Britt Davis was never going to bend.

When she didn't respond, Phil walked away with Dillon, who was now screaming at the top of his lungs, holding his arms toward his mother. She stood as if turned to stone.

"Britt," Quinn murmured in a low voice, wanting to say something, anything, to take that look from her face.

She leveled that angry gaze on him and slammed the door in his face.

Chapter Six

How dare he!

Britt would never speak to Quinn again. He was of no concern to her now.

Her emotions overtook her and she slid down to collapse on the floor. The tears she'd been holding in check burst forth like water from a broken pipe. Her stomach cramped with nausea and she drew up her knees to stop the pain. Loud, heart-wrenching sobs echoed around the room, but not even her anguish could block out Dillon's pitiful wails.

I'm sorry, baby. Mommy didn't protect you. Mommy screwed up.

She wasn't sure how long she sat there in her agony. It could have been a few minutes or an hour. Finally, she raised her head and wiped away tears with the back of her hand. She had to get her son back and would start her quest this instant. Pushing herself to her feet, she headed for her phone. It rang before she reached it.

Her mother, Britt knew without a doubt.

"Hi, Mom," she said into the receiver, trying to sound as cheerful as possible.

"Are you okay?"

"Emotionally I'm a little ragged, but I'll be fine."

"Oh, baby."

"I've decided to quit my job," she blurted.

"Oh. That's rather sudden."

"It's the only way I can get Dillon back. I'll find somethin' else."

"Whatever you feel is best."

She could always count on her mom for support.

"Why don't you come home and stay for a few days until you get used—"

"Thanks, Mom, but I have a lot to do. I'm calling my supervisor as soon as I get off the phone with you, and I'll probably fly to New York tomorrow to turn in my ID and manuals. I'm sure I'll have papers to sign."

"It just breaks my heart what that man has done to you."

Britt bit her lip. "He fooled me, but another man will never get that chance. If anything, I'm tougher and wiser."

"Oh, sweetie, would you like for me to come over?" Britt could hear the worry in her mother's voice. It hurt that she'd caused her so much anguish. Carin had wanted her to stay in college and get her degree, but Britt had had a friend who was leaving college to attend an airline attendant program. Seeing the world was a dream come true, and when the semester ended, Britt had joined her friend. She'd never regretted her decision. Until now.

That's how she'd met Phil—on a flight to London with a lady friend. He'd flirted shamelessly in front of the woman, and had called Britt when they were back in the States. He'd never told her how he got her number. By devious means, she was sure. She was so gullible. She'd never seen the warning signs, and she should have.

"Britt, are you there?"

It took her a moment to gather her thoughts. "Mom, I'm fine. I'll call you later."

"Okay. Oh, have you heard from Mama today?"

"No, why?"

"She wasn't here this morning when I got up. I thought she was working in that ridiculous winter garden, but when I checked she wasn't. She was on the phone with Enzo a long time last night, and I have a suspicion that she caught a bus to go see him."

"Didn't y'all stop by yesterday?"

"No, I was too upset."

"Just call Uncle Enzo."

"I did, but he doesn't answer. Sometimes he doesn't hear the phone. I better start looking. I swear she's worse than a child."

"If she shows up, I'll call you."

"Phone me anyway. I want to hear from you."

Britt's doorbell rang. "Gotta go. Someone's here."

"Call if it's Mama."

Britt walked to the door, hoping it was Onnie. Her grandmother being out on her own could not be good for anyone.

"Britt, I'd like to talk to you," a voice said loudly.

She stopped in her tracks. *Quinn*.

"I have nothing to say to you—ever."

"Just five minutes."

"If you don't leave, I'm calling the police."

She pressed her ear against the door. *Silence*. He was gone.

Resting her head against the wood, she allowed herself to think about him. She had really liked him—his humor, his bravery—and had felt an attraction, a connection she'd never experienced before. She'd trusted him.

But her hero was one of the bad guys.

When would she ever learn?

Curling her hands into fists, she marched back to the

phone to call her lawyer. Mona needed to hear her decision, and then Britt would call her supervisor. She had a full day ahead of her.

And maybe somewhere in the busyness she wouldn't hear Dillon crying.

Or see Quinn's face. Or hear his voice.

QUINN HURRIED INTO HIS office, his stomach tied into a tight reef knot. He had only wanted to talk, but Britt wasn't willing to listen to any explanations. He had crossed a line by going back without his client. But he'd crossed lines before.

He just wanted to make sure she was okay, even though he knew she wasn't. There was nothing left to say and he had to accept that.

His secretary, Denise, handed him some messages and walked out. Levi Coyote, his P.I., lounged in a chair, his long legs stretched out, his cowboy boots crossed at the ankles. A Stetson, pulled low, hid his expression, but Quinn knew he wasn't asleep. Levi was part Indian and he didn't know what else, but the man had better tracking and hunting skills than anyone he'd ever met.

They'd attended the same high school, two young lads as different as night and day. Quinn was a city boy, Levi country, but somewhere they'd made a connection. Quinn helped Levi with his homework, and Levi taught him how to be tough. After graduation, they went their separate ways. Levi attended the academy and became a police officer. Quinn went to law school. When Quinn became a defense attorney he'd needed a good P.I. He'd heard that Levi had left the department and was doing investigative work. One phone call was all it took for them to connect again. Levi had worked for him ever since.

As Quinn laid his briefcase on the desk, Levi sat up

straight, his dark eyes alert. "What's up? Your secretary called."

Quinn opened his briefcase, pulled out the folder with the photos of Britt and placed them on the desk in front of his friend. "I want you to verify these."

Levi flipped through the pictures. He didn't ask questions or comment. Quinn liked that about Levi. He was very straightforward. "Just so we're clear, explain 'verify.'"

"I want to know Ms. Davis's involvement with the men in the pictures and when, where and how that condo was trashed."

Levi stood. "Consider it done."

"I need the info as soon as possible."

"You always do." His friend headed for the door.

"This is important."

Levi looked back with his hand on the doorknob, one eyebrow lifted slightly beneath the brim of his hat. "Aren't they all?"

Quinn shrugged. "This one more than most."

He nodded and walked through the door just before Quinn's assistant, Steve Archer, walked in.

"The Bailey case is on the docket at the end of November."

"Good." Quinn opened his laptop. "I have a meeting with the D.A. next week and I'm hoping to get a plea bargain. Jerry Bailey doesn't need to be in prison. He needs help."

"Good luck with that. He did kill his stepfather." Steve was a skeptic about most things.

Quinn leaned back. "Lloyd Dixon was an abusive drunk who repeatedly beat his wife and her two kids. Jerry shot him trying to stop him from beating and raping his sister. I think he deserves a medal."

"If I know you, you'll make sure he gets it."

Steve was fresh out of law school and tended to cast Quinn as a hero, whereas many people vilified defense attorneys. But Quinn only took cases where he felt the defendant was innocent or being railroaded by the D.A.'s office. It was well known that if Quinn took a case, he'd done his homework, and the D.A. had a fight on his hands. These days the D.A.'s office usually listened to him. Not that he always got his way, but he was in there fighting.

Denise popped her head around the corner. "Deidre has called three times. Those messages are from her."

"Are you saying I should call her back?" Quinn asked in a teasing tone.

"Please." She placed her hands on her hips. "Or I'll just answer the phone all day."

He winked. "I'll do it right away. And I'll need someone to oversee the Rutherford case."

"We're babysitting now?" Steve asked with a touch of cynicism.

"Anything the judge orders." Quinn dropped his voice. "Got it?"

"Yes, sir. I was—"

Quinn held up a hand. "Never mind. If I need you at the Rutherford condo, you'll be there."

"Yes, sir."

"This might be a good job for Bea or Gail," Denise ventured. "They like babies."

"Set it up. Whoever it is has to be there at eight on Sunday morning, and, of course, she'll be off on Monday."

"Will do." Denise headed back to her office.

And Quinn's day went on, chaotic and stressful. Through it all he was haunted by Britt's sad, dark eyes.

BRITT MET WITH MONA AFTER lunch. Her firm was located in an old house off Congress Avenue that had been converted into offices. It was pleasant, with lots of green plants and homey touches like candles and fluffy pillows.

Britt sat in a comfy chair gripping a pillow printed with bright red flowers.

"Are you sure you want to quit your job?" Mona was seated at her white French provincial desk.

"I've been dissatisfied for months with being away from Dillon. I should have quit long ago, and today might not have happened."

Mona pushed back her blond hair with a weary hand. "I don't think so. I got the feeling Mr. Wallis and Mr. Ross had all sorts of ammunition to fire at us. The judge had already made up her mind, though, which is a little suspicious to me." She touched legal papers on her desk. "I'm drafting an appeal and thinking about filing a complaint against Judge Norcutt. A woman's job shouldn't matter. Her mothering capabilities should. The judge didn't want to hear anything I had to say."

Mona was a fighter and Britt liked that about her. "How long will an appeal take?"

"Too long, so I suppose quitting your job is the best solution. But it bugs the crap out of me that we have to cave in to the judge's antiquated ideas."

"I just want my baby." Britt stood. "I'm flying to New York in the morning to do the necessary paperwork. I'll start job hunting when I get back. You have my cell number if you need to contact me."

"Hang in there, Britt."

"I'm trying."

As Britt was leaving the office, her mother called.

"I finally found Mama," Carin said.

"Where was she?" Britt walked out the door to her car.

"At Enzo's. Evidently, he called early this morning and

said he was sick. Strange I didn't hear the phone. Anyway, she took him chicken soup and said she might stay the night."

"Why didn't she tell you?"

"She insisted she left a note, but I can't find it."

"Mom, this sounds strange." Britt slid into her car.

"I know. I promised Vera I'd sit with her mother today so she could have a day off, but I plan to pick up Mama later. She can't spend the night. It's not allowed."

Britt's mom was always there for everyone. Vera was a neighbor whose mother had had a stroke, and Carin helped out when she could. When Britt was growing up, Carin had been a stay-at-home mom and a homemaker, and she still was. Her husband's death had shaken them all, and Britt thought getting a job might help Carin. Instead, she continued to help others. And she didn't need to work. Ten years ago her husband's car had been hit by an eighteen wheeler whose brakes had malfunctioned. The company made a large financial settlement, enabling Britt to go to college and Carin to take care of Onnie and anyone else who needed it. Her mother was very frugal, making the money last. How Britt wished she had been more like her mom—being there for her child. She pushed the thought away, resolving to be there from now on.

Backing out of the parking lot, she asked, "Do you want me to check on them?"

"No, you have enough to deal with."

"I have an early flight so I'll talk to you when I get back."

"Okay, baby, and try not to worry."

That was almost impossible, Britt decided as she drove home. Inside the apartment she picked up a few of Dillon's toys, holding them to her chest for a moment before putting them away. Her heart ached and tears weren't far off. And it was only the first day. How was she going to survive four months without her baby?

AFTER LOSING A LOT OF THE morning dealing with the Rutherford case, Quinn was working late. Deidre wanted to spend the weekend on her dad's houseboat on Lake Austin. He wanted to make sure Sunday went smoothly for Britt, so he refused to join Deidre, using work as an excuse, even though it ticked her off. But it wasn't really an excuse. He had to get all his ducks in a row for his meeting with the D.A. in the Bailey case. For every argument he wanted to have a counterargument.

A shuffling sound interrupted his thoughts. All his employees had gone for the day and it was too early for the cleaning crew. He heard muffled voices. Clearly, someone was in the outer office. Getting up, he walked around his desk to the door. He paused as he saw two elderly people, a man and a woman. Evidently they were lost.

"Are you sure this is it, Ona?" the man asked. He was tall, thin, stooped over and was completely bald. The woman was just the opposite, short and round with gray permed hair, support hose and a large purse on one arm. Their backs were to him.

Quinn stepped forward. "May I help you?"

The woman swung around, the man more slowly. Quinn froze. In the man's hand was a gun. And it was pointed at Quinn.

"What the…"

"Are you Quentin Ross?" the woman asked in a direct, no-nonsense voice.

Quinn stared at the gun. It looked big, old and heavy, and he could swear it had rust on it.

"What are you doing in here and what are you doing with that gun?"

"Now listen here, mister." The woman moved closer, her brown eyes narrowed on him. "I'll ask the questions, and if you know what's good for you, you'll answer them."

Had they escaped from a home or something? An asylum maybe? This was bizarre.

"Are you Quentin Ross?" the woman asked again, her voice angry now.

Despite the gun, the two looked fairly harmless. Maybe they just needed a lawyer. "Yes. I'm Quentin Ross."

"Figured you'd be some slick sonobitch." She flicked a glance over his suit, white shirt and tie as if she was looking at dog poop.

"What?" He was taken aback by the vicious words.

"Listen up. You're gonna do exactly what we tell you or Enzo's gonna shoot you."

Quinn's body tightened. He wasn't afraid, just getting more annoyed by the minute. "What would that be?"

"Give Britt back her baby—tonight."

Britt.

Then it dawned on him. The infamous grandmother.

"I don't have Britt's baby. He's with his father."

"But you made it happen. Now make it unhappen."

"Ma'am…" He took a step toward her, hoping to make her understand.

She moved back. "Don't come a step closer or Enzo will shoot."

At that precise moment they heard a snore, and both of them glanced at Enzo. Standing there, he'd fallen asleep, his chin on his chest, the gun still in his hand.

"Enzo!" the woman shouted.

He blinked and looked around. "Did we find him?"

"You idiot." She jerked the ancient gun from his hand. "I thought I could depend on you."

"You can, Ona, but I'm tired after walking up all those stairs."

"Why didn't you take the elevator?" Quinn asked.

"Because we didn't want anyone to see us, that's why, hotshot." The woman waved the gun at him. "Now are you going to do what we want?"

Enzo appeared shaky, and Quinn grabbed his arm before he collapsed. "Here." He pulled out a chair. "Have a seat."

"Bless you, son. That's mighty nice."

"He's not nice, Enzo," Ona yelled. "He's the lawyer who took Britt's baby."

"You sonobitch. You shouldn't have done that. Now we're gonna have to hurt you," her companion stated.

The man couldn't hurt a cockroach. But Quinn wasn't so sure about Ona.

"Enzo, you're looking a little pale." Britt's grandmother tucked the gun under her arm and opened her suitcase of a purse. "Probably low blood sugar. Here." She handed him a candy bar. "Eat this."

Quinn knew he could overpower them at any time, but he decided to let this play out. Just to humor them. And that was the most insane thing he'd ever done, except for jumping into a swollen creek to save her granddaughter.

Enzo took a bite and glanced at him. "Got any beer?"

Quinn had liquor in his office, but he wasn't offering it to Enzo. That was the last thing the man needed. "No. But I have water. Just a minute." He went into the small kitchen off Denise's office and found a bottle of water. He glanced at the phone, knowing he could call the police. But he wasn't sure what that would accomplish. And he didn't relish the thought of putting Britt's grandmother in jail, even if she was off her rocker.

When he returned, Ona had pulled up a chair next to Enzo, the gun and purse in her lap. He removed the cap and handed Enzo the water, and then carefully reached over for the gun.

But Ona was too quick. She jerked it away. "Not so fast, hotshot." She pointed the weapon at his chest.

"I don't think that rusty gun will fire," he told her, not batting an eye.

"Wanna find out?" A gleam entered her eyes similar to one he'd seen in Britt's.

"Fired in 1945," Enzo said, munching on the candy bar.

"Go ahead then, shoot me." Quinn held out his arms, thinking the only way to deal with insanity was with more insanity.

Chapter Seven

Quinn and Ona stared at each other.

Her eyes squinted down the barrel of the gun. "You don't think I will, do you?"

"No, ma'am." He lowered his arms. "You wouldn't shoot a man in cold blood."

"Don't be too sure about that, hotshot. My Britt's heart is broken and I aim to change that."

Enzo choked, gasping for air. Ona laid the gun on her purse and slapped him on the back.

"Goddamn nuts," Enzo choked out, his eyes watery. "You know I can't eat nuts with my false teeth."

"Good heavens, they're just little bitty things."

"But you know—"

"Give it a rest, Enzo."

While they were arguing, Quinn reached down and slowly removed the gun, slipping it into Denise's desk drawer without either of them noticing.

Enzo took a big swallow of water and handed him the bottle. "I'd rather have beer."

Ona looked around and then directly at him. "Did you take my gun?"

"Yes, I did, and you're not getting it back."

"Listen here…" She started to rise, but Enzo caught her arm.

"Leave it alone, Ona. We can't kill nobody. I tried to tell you that." The old man stared at Quinn through his thick bifocals. "But I have mob connections and I can get someone to take him out."

Quinn crossed his arms over his chest. "You have mob connections?"

"As a boy in Chicago I ran errands for the mob, and I still have connections."

"So you see, you better give Britt her baby." Ona was big on threats.

Quinn's patience was wearing thin. "Okay, now listen. This is only a separation. Britt will have her baby back soon. And you don't need to hurt anyone to accomplish that."

"But not quick enough," Ona wailed, a tear sparkling in her eye. Quinn would have sworn that this tougher-than-nails woman never cried.

"I'm Phil Rutherford's lawyer, so I can't say anything else. Just rest assured things will change." Quinn wasn't making empty promises. He planned to get to the bottom of the custody hearing.

"See, I told you he's a nice man," Enzo said.

"You're so gullible." Ona pursed her lips, not convinced.

Enzo leaned forward. "Do you know if a bus runs by here at this hour? I'm ready for bed."

Quinn sighed. "I'll see if I can get you a ride home."

"We don't need your help," Ona retorted.

"Yes, we do." Enzo overruled her. "It's past my bedtime."

"You sleep all the damn time."

"I'm ninety-two and I can damn well sleep anytime I want to, missy."

"Mob connection, ha!" Quinn heard Ona say as he walked into his office, letting them argue.

He sat at his desk and opened the Rutherford file. Britt's number was in there, and he had to call her. If she didn't answer, or hung up on him, he'd have to take Bonnie and Clyde home. Leaving them to their own devices at this time of night would be dangerous.

Punching in Britt's number, he waited. And waited. Evidently she had caller ID and wasn't taking his calls. Damn it! She was one stubborn woman, and he knew exactly where she got if from—the fireball in his reception area.

"If you'd have bought me beer like I asked, this would have gone better." The argument was still going on.

"You'd have been drunk on your ass," Ona retorted.

"You're becoming one bitchy old woman, Ona."

"Old? I'm nine years younger than you!"

"That ain't saying much."

Quinn slipped into his black coat and noticed that neither Bonnie nor Clyde had a jacket. It had been fifty degrees earlier, and the temperature was dropping.

"Where are your coats?"

"Don't need one," Ona replied.

"Forgot them at my place," Enzo replied. "Ona has a head like a rock."

"Shut up, Enzo."

Slowly, they made their way to the elevator. Quinn decided that Enzo really needed a cane, and he wondered if they'd forgotten that, too. He made them wait in front of the building while he went to the parking area to get his car. Enzo couldn't walk any farther, and Quinn wanted to get them out of the weather as soon as possible.

When he pulled up to the curb, both of them were shivering. He just shook his head and helped them into his

Mercedes, which was nice and warm. Before he drove two blocks, Enzo was asleep, snoring.

Quinn had to wake him at his assisted living facility. With his and Ona's help, Enzo made it to his room. The place had a distinct smell and it wasn't pleasant. A sad fact of life. At least Enzo was able to get around and go on crazy missions with Ona. Dim lights lit the hallway and the sound of coughing could be heard, but otherwise everything was quiet.

Inside, Enzo said, "I missed my supper."

"I'll fix you something," Ona offered, and hurried to the compact refrigerator in a corner. Enzo sank onto the twin bed and was instantly asleep again.

"He's out," Quinn said to Ona.

She closed the refrigerator and came over to Enzo. Lifting his feet onto the bed, she removed his worn tennis shoes, jerked a quilt from a recliner and covered him. She kissed his forehead. "'Night, Enzo. I'll call you tomorrow. Don't worry, we'll think of something else."

Back in the car, Quinn asked Ona, "You didn't mean that, did you?"

"What?"

"About somethin' else."

She pulled the wool coat she'd retrieved from Enzo's room tighter around her. "I'm not going to rest until Dillon is with his mother again."

"Give the court some time to work."

"Harrumph."

"I'm not trying to hurt your granddaughter."

"Coulda fooled me."

"Try having a little faith and trust."

She turned slightly in the darkness of the car and he felt those razor sharp eyes slicing into him. "I stopped believing and trusting the day my son was killed in Vietnam."

"I'm sorry." Quinn remembered Britt saying something about her grandmother's losses in life. It certainly had hardened her.

"Don't be. If the gun had worked, you'd be a dead dirtbag."

"You never pulled the trigger."

"Minor technicality." Ona looked out at the traffic and at the buildings they were passing. "Are you taking me to the warden?"

"Who's that?"

"My daughter."

"I'm taking you to Britt's."

"Good. The lecture won't be as severe. Carin can ramble on for days."

He pulled up to Britt's apartment complex. It was a newer brick building in a good area of Austin. A small children's playground was to the left. That must have been one of its selling features for Britt. Another pang of regret hit him at his involvement in the case.

Turning off the engine, he asked, "Ready to face the music?"

There was a long pause. "A baby should be with his mother." The words came out low and hoarse.

"Yes, ma'am. God willing, that will happen soon."

"It never would have happened if you hadn't represented that low-life sleazebag." She opened her door. "I hope you can live with yourself."

He sighed. That was becoming harder and harder.

BRITT PACKED WHAT SHE needed in a carryall. She'd didn't plan to spend the night. The sooner she was back in Austin the better.

Her doorbell rang and she went to answer it, looking through the peephole first. Her mother. Britt quickly opened the door.

"I can't find Mama anywhere," Carin said, walking in and removing her coat.

Britt closed the door. "She's not at Enzo's?"

"No." Carin sank onto the sofa, placing her purse beside her. "Uncle Enzo's not there, either. The lady at the home said he was there earlier and Mama was visiting him, but they don't know where they are now." Carin gripped her hands together in her lap. "Where are they, Britt? And what are they up to? I keep waiting for a call."

She sat by her mother and hugged her. "Is the home looking for them?"

"Mrs. Gaston said they would, but—"

The doorbell rang.

"I'll get it, and please stay calm. We'll find them even if I have to cancel my flight."

"You have enough to worry about."

"It's no worry. I love Onnie."

Britt hurried to the door and once again looked through the peephole. Him again!

"Go away. I'm not talking to you."

Carin got to her feet. "Who is it?"

"No one who matters."

"This is not a social call. Your grandmother is with me."

What? Britt yanked open the door. "Onnie, where have you been?"

"Mama." Carin hurried to confront her mother. "I've been worried out of my mind."

"You're always worried." Ona shrugged out of her coat.

"Where have you been?" Carin demanded.

"Somethin' had to be done, so Enzo and I decided to kill Quentin Ross."

Carin fainted.

"Mom!" Britt screamed, and knelt beside her. "Mom. Mom!"

Quinn bent to help. "Don't touch my mother," she growled in a low voice.

They eyed each other over her prone body for a second. Britt was angry and wanted him out of her apartment. His eyes flashed a blue warning. Looking away, he lifted Carin's head. "Mrs. Davis."

"Oo-o-o-h." She reached for her forehead.

"Are you okay?" Britt helped her sit up. Quinn held on to her, too. Britt shot him a go-to-hell glance.

"Did Mama say…?"

"It's okay, Mrs. Davis," Quinn murmured. "As you can see, I'm alive."

"He wouldn't be if I had my way." Onnie sat with her arms crossed over her chest, a stubborn expression Britt knew well firmly in place.

"Have you lost your mind? What were you thinking?" Carin was recovering, going into full rant.

"I was thinking of helping my granddaughter. That bastard took her baby." Onnie pointed at Quinn, unmoved by Carin's anger. "Somebody had to do somethin'. Dillon needs to be here, with his mother. With us." Her voice wavered on the last word and Britt went to her.

Sitting beside her, she gave her a hug. "You know, I thought about killing him myself—with my bare hands." Her eyes held Quinn's as she said the words.

The blue eyes darkened and she knew she'd hit a nerve.

"Hot damn. Now we're talking."

"Britt!" Carin gasped.

"But I don't want to go to prison. I just want Dillon home."

"Me, too," Onnie said under her breath, and Britt hugged her again.

"Tell me what happened," Britt suggested, rubbing her arm.

"Let the hotshot attorney tell you."

Britt glanced at Quinn. For a moment she didn't think he was going to say anything, but then he began to speak.

"Enzo and Ona showed up at my office earlier with a gun, threatening to shoot me if I didn't get Dillon back. I explained it was the judge's decision, not mine and—"

"Oh, but you had a big hand in it, didn't you." Britt got to her feet, unable to stop the words she'd kept locked inside and sworn she would never say to him. Not one word. But…

"I didn't know you were Roslyn Davis." He got that in before she could finish her tirade.

"It didn't stop you, though, did it? You stood there and took my child even after all the bad things I told you about Phil. You put my baby in his care. How could you do that? How could you do that to Dillon? To me?"

"I was honor bound—"

"Shove your honor," she shouted, and her mother touched her arm.

"Sweetie, do you know Mr. Ross?"

Britt gulped a breath. "Regrettably, yes. He's the man who pulled me from the flooded creek."

"Oh, my goodness." Carin placed a hand on her chest.

"And I almost shot him," Ona quipped.

"You couldn't pull the trigger, Ona," Quinn told her. "The gun is still at my office. I'd appreciate it if someone could pick it up tomorrow."

"Throw it away," Carin instructed. "I never want to see that thing again."

"Now wait a minute." Onnie was on her feet.

"Throw it away," Carin said again. "It's time for us to go home. It's getting late."

Carin and Ona slipped into their coats. "I'm going to put an alarm on the front and back doors so I know when you're leaving," Carin informed her mother.

"Why don't you put bars on the windows, too?"

"I might." Carin kissed Britt. "I'll talk to you tomorrow." She looked at Quinn. "I don't know what to say to you, Mr. Ross, so I'll say nothing. Let's go, Mama."

Britt kissed her grandmother and the door closed, leaving her and Quinn alone. She walked back into the living area, which suddenly seemed smaller than usual due to Quinn's overpowering presence.

"You can leave," she murmured.

"Not until I've said my piece."

"Oh, please." She wrapped her arms around her waist as if to ward off any attraction she might feel.

"Family law is not my field. It was when I first started, but then I switched to defense. Phil and I were in law school together. We weren't close, just acquaintances with the same classes and same friends. Philip Sr. gave me my start, and I worked for his law firm for several years. I've always been grateful for that. When Phil called me to take over for his ailing attorney, I agreed. The file on Roslyn Davis was very clear—she was a bad mother leaving her child for long periods of time."

"How dare you!"

"I'm telling you what was in the file. That's not my opinion."

Their eyes locked and she saw the concern, the empathy in his eyes. No! She would not weaken.

But she found herself asking, "What's your opinion?"

"I believe what you told me in the woods."

Unbelievable relief flooded her, surprising her. Why should she care? But she couldn't deny that she did.

"It doesn't change anything, though. I am now Phil's lawyer of record for this case."

She stiffened. "Then we have nothing else to say to each other."

"I'm breaking the rules by even talking to you."

"Then leave."

But he didn't. He kept staring at her with those blue, blue eyes. "I find that hard to do," he admitted in a hoarse voice.

Could her life get any crazier? They were pulled together by emotions and torn apart by circumstances out of their control.

She swallowed. "Thank you for not calling the police on my grandmother and Enzo."

"It's kind of hard to have Bonnie and Clyde arrested." A twinkle was back in his eyes.

"Bonnie and Clyde?"

"That's my name for them. Kind of fits, don't you think?"

"Mmm."

"I really thought you were exaggerating about your grandmother."

"No, Onnie's in a class all her own."

"Yeah." He slipped his hands into the pockets of his slacks, drawing her attention to his long, lean body, and from out of nowhere she remembered the feel of his lips on hers, that hard form pressed into hers. Her breath caught in her throat.

"I think it's wise if we don't see each other outside of the courtroom."

"That's probably best." But he didn't move or make an attempt to leave. They kept staring at each other as if their eyes could say what they couldn't. He cleared his throat. "Someone from my office will meet with you at eight on Sunday morning at Phil's condo."

"I'll be there."

"Britt..."

The entreaty in his voice sent her nerves spinning, but she maintained her dignity. And that was about all she had left. "Please, we've said enough."

He nodded and headed for the door, stopping at her side. "I'm sorry things turned out this way."

A tangy, manly scent reached her nostrils. She resisted the temptation to fill her system with the taste of him. If she turned, their faces would be inches apart. So close. So tempting.

She couldn't. Wouldn't. She bit her lip as he walked out the door.

Chapter Eight

Quinn was back in his office early the next morning. He retrieved the gun from Denise's desk and placed it in the safe until he figured out what to do with it. The thing was as rusty as a nail left out in the rain. The chamber wouldn't even move. Bonnie and Clyde couldn't even see that the gun was no longer usable. But it had worked for their purpose—getting his attention.

Last night, he'd thought of telling them they were trying to shoot the wrong man—that Phil should be their target. But then they might actually try to kill him. Quinn hoped it never occurred to them to go after Phil because he would most definitely have them arrested.

Quinn's own grandparents had been quite sane, so he'd never met anyone like Ona. Britt's life must have been entertaining, at best.

Britt.

Last night he'd wanted to touch her, to take the pain from her eyes and to explore all those feelings he'd experienced in the woods. No woman had ever made him feel like that—an all-conquering male who could move mountains. The gulf was so wide between them now that any relationship was out of the question. That's why he'd left, when he'd wanted to linger.

And then there was Deidre.

He sighed, wondering why he hadn't heard from her. Anytime he'd canceled on her, she'd usually pout for a few days and then call as if everything was fine. Soon he'd have to decide about his relationship with her. If they even had one.

His cell buzzed. He looked at the caller ID. His sister. He clicked on.

"Hey, sis, what are you doing up so early?"

"Remember? I have a one-year-old."

"Oh, yeah. How is J.W.?"

"He's awake and helping Jody get dressed for school."

"Mommy!" Quinn could hear Jody shouting in the background.

"I guess he's helping a little too much. I have to go, but I wanted to see if you can come for dinner on Sunday."

"Sorry, sis, I have plans."

"Please tell me you've met someone."

"No, just business plans." But Britt's face was right there at the front of his mind.

"Mommy!" This time Jody was screaming.

"Bye," Peyton said, and hung up.

Quinn laid his phone on the desk, feeling a pang of envy. His sister was happy. He was glad one of them had found happiness. Home and family. The older he got the more important those two things became. But as he'd told Britt, he'd probably wind up a crusty old bachelor.

His career always came first and he'd worked hard to get where he was. The Rutherfords were now jeopardizing that success. As long as they could pull his strings everything was fine, but how long could he allow that? Philip Sr. had deep pockets and long arms when it came to the Texas Bar Association. At the first sign of an ethical violation, he would have Quinn disbarred in the blink of an eye.

Quinn shifted uneasily in his chair. He didn't like anyone having that much power over his career. Over *him*.

A tap at the door brought him out of his thoughts.

"Yes," he called.

Levi walked in with a folder in his hand. It wasn't unusual for the investigator to be here early. If he was working a case, he was sometimes in the office before Quinn.

Levi slapped the folder on the desk. "That was a piece of cake."

"What do you mean?"

He sank into a chair and crossed one booted foot over his knee. "The men were easy to locate and willing to talk."

"And?"

In one swift movement Levi was on his feet and had opened the folder. It always surprised Quinn how fast he could move.

"This man—" Levi poked one photo "—is a New York businessman with dealings in the Middle East. He has two boys, ages two and four. He and Ms. Davis had dinner during a layover and talked about their children. Same with the pilot from Atlanta and the race car driver from Italy. They talked about their kids—that's it. And they were not happy that photos had been taken of them. But none of them were worried, since they all have secure, happy marriages. All three had told their wives about Ms. Davis and how she made their time away from their families so much easier."

Just as Quinn had suspected. "And the trashed condo?"

"No police report. Nothing. That was a dead end. But I used a computer program to blow up the photos, and if you'll look closely—" he pulled out two large photos "—you'll see there's a lamp knocked over and women's clothes thrown on the floor. Nothing else is disturbed."

He pointed to the other photo. "This is in a bedroom. The bedding is all tumbled up and grocery items are strewn around. You can see a busted bag, a box of long candles, unopened, French bread, a salad mix, a piece of meat—looks like prime rib—and two potatoes. Nothing else is disturbed. If you ask me, it appears as if someone dropped the bag. I wouldn't call that trashing a condo."

"Thanks, Levi. This helps a lot." Everything was just as he suspected. Britt was being railroaded, and Quinn knew without a doubt that the Rutherfords were not planning to give Dillon back to his mother. And they would use Quinn as long as he allowed it. He had to bide his time and gather more evidence. When Philip Sr. made his move, Quinn had to be prepared.

"One more thing," he said as Levi made to leave. "Ms. Davis is being tailed. I want to know who, and who hired him."

"Sure." Levi rubbed his chin. "Is this personal?"

"Yes." Quinn surprised himself with the answer. It felt good to admit that out loud.

Levi hesitated, which was unlike him. He was a man who did his job and didn't ask questions. "Ms. Davis is very beautiful."

Quinn looked up. "It's more than that."

Levi raised his hands. "I'm not prying or giving advice, but you're Phil Rutherford's attorney."

"Yeah." Quinn leaned back in his leather chair. "That does present a problem."

"You wouldn't be the first man to lose his head over a woman."

"Have you?" Quinn lifted an eyebrow.

"Hell, no. I have more sense than that."

The quick denial told Quinn that he had.

"Just be careful," Levi added. "The Rutherfords have a lot of power in this town. In this state."

Quinn nodded; he knew that better than anyone. He leaned forward. "Damn, Levi, this is the first time we've had a personal conversation."

"And let's keep it that way," his colleague replied with a half grin. "Just know I have your back...and your ass."

"Thanks. Oh, don't you want Ms. Davis's address?"

"I wouldn't be much of a detective if I didn't already have it." With that, Levi sauntered out the door.

BRITT FLEW TO NEW YORK and did what she had to. Her friends, Wendy and Donna, were getting ready for a flight, and she was glad for the chance to say goodbye. They hated to see her go, but understood. She didn't linger in the city she loved. She didn't see a Broadway show, shop, stroll through Times Square or visit Central Park. Her focus wasn't in New York anymore. It was in Austin— with Dillon.

When she arrived back, she quickly packed a bag and drove to Taylor to spend the weekend with her mother and Onnie. Britt couldn't stay in the apartment without Dillon, even though she knew she would eventually have to. But not this weekend.

The main purpose of the visit was to talk to her grandmother. Onnie had to understand how wrong she had been to try to hurt Quinn. But talking to Onnie was sometimes like talking to a wall. Britt didn't need any more aggravation, and neither did her mother, so for all their sakes, she hoped Onnie would listen to her.

She planned to stay Friday night and soothe ruffled feathers, and come home on Saturday to get ready for her day with her son. She hoped he was settling in and not missing her. Her focus was on this Sunday, when she'd be able to see and hold her baby. That was all Britt could think about. She would make the most of her time with Dillon. Until the next time. Until he was with her again.

QUINN HAD THE CONVERSATION with Deidre, but it wasn't fun. She'd called from the lake to tell him that since he was so busy, she'd invited another man. Quinn hated when she tried to make him jealous. He told her to have a good time, and she became angrier, telling him this was it. They were over. He agreed and she hung up on him.

Staring at the phone, he wondered why some women had to manipulate, to control. He was so tired of the endless tug-of-war between them. It was time for it to end. And, oddly, he wasn't upset.

Denise walked in and handed him a letter. "This just came by courier."

"Thanks." He ripped open the envelope and a check fell out. For twenty thousand dollars. His stomach clenched and he glanced at the attached letter: *Quinn, I appreciate your help in securing my grandson's future. Your loyalty will not go unnoticed. Enjoy the bonus.* It was signed by Philip Sr.

"Son of a bitch!"

Quinn grabbed a page of letterhead stationery and scribbled a note that read thanks but no thanks. Slipping the check inside, he sealed the envelope and shouted for Denise.

She ran in, her eyes huge. "What? What?"

Handing her the letter, he said, "Get this back to Philip Rutherford Sr. as soon as possible."

"Oh, okay. I thought there was a fire in here."

"Take care of the letter," Quinn snapped.

She hurried away and he sucked in a deep breath, the air burning his lungs. Damn! He hit the desk with his fist, the sound echoing in his ears. The Rutherfords were setting him up to take Britt's baby—forever. He knew that without any doubt. It was time to pay the piper.

Standing, he stretched the tight muscles in his shoulders. When Quinn's interest had turned to defense, Philip had supported his decision. After courtroom training and several more law classes, he'd joined the Rutherford defense team, but it wasn't quite his niche. Quinn disliked the expensive retainers and the total lack of respect for the victims. He'd wanted his own firm, to do things his way. Philip had again supported him, sending him clients when his own team was backlogged. Without that help, Quinn wouldn't be where he was today.

How much was that support worth?

His soul?

Guilt scraped across his conscience and he couldn't breathe. He needed air, freedom. Grabbing his coat, he headed for the door. "Cancel my appointments for the afternoon," he said to Denise. "Reschedule for Monday."

"What?"

But he wasn't listening. He hit the stairwell, slipping into his coat. In a matter of minutes he was in his car, driving out of Austin toward Horseshoe, Texas. And his sister.

It was ironic that as an adult he turned to her for advice. In their youth, Peyton had always been running to him.

Right now, Quinn had to face his options and make the right decision for himself.

And for Britt.

AN HOUR AND A HALF LATER he sat in the living room of the large Victorian house Peyton and Wyatt had renovated. J.W. sat on his lap, holding a worn teddy bear, listening to a story Quinn was reading. Peyton and Wyatt were curled up on the sofa side by side, watching them.

Jody ran in in her pajamas and fuzzy slippers, followed by her yellow Lab, Doolittle. "I'm ready for bed," she announced.

Wyatt stood and lifted a sleeping J.W. out of his arms. Quinn never realized how good it felt to hold a child. He could only imagine Britt's torment at not having her son with her.

"Time for bed, kiddos," his brother-in-law said. "Daddy will put you to bed."

"What about Mommy?" Jody asked.

"Mommy is visiting with Uncle Quinn."

"Oh." The little girl ran to Peyton and kissed her. "'Night, Mommy, and don't forget Erin's coming for a sleepover tomorrow. Love you."

"How could I forget?" Peyton kissed her daughter. "I love you, too. I'll check on you later."

Jody hugged Quinn. "I'm glad you surprised us."

"'Night, Jody." He hugged her back.

Wyatt, the kids and Doolittle walked up the stairs. Quinn watched them go and then concentrated on the crackling fire. He rarely lit the fireplace at his house, and tonight he found looking at the flames warm and soothing. Calming.

Peyton got up and sat cross-legged in front of the fire, facing him. The flames behind her highlighted her blonde hair, and she gazed at him in concern.

"What's going on, Quinn? You said you were busy and now you're here."

And just like that he told her everything that had happened since the flood.

When he'd finished, she stood, and he knew that look on her face. He'd seen it may times when she was younger. She was angry.

"That stupid judge took her child?"

"Yes."

"And you let it happen?"

He swallowed. "Yes."

"Quentin Ross, I can't believe you'd do such a thing."

"Haven't you listened to anything I've said? They're setting me up and they're framing Britt."

"You're the best lawyer I know. You can change things."

"I'm the Rutherfords' attorney. If I do anything to thwart their plans, I'll lose my license. And Philip Sr. will make sure I never practice law again—anywhere."

"So it comes down to what you value more—your career or your conscience. Can you live with yourself if you take that baby from his mother?"

Quinn looked down at his hands, clasped between his legs. Peyton had a way of getting to the point, and the truth dug into him.

"I think this has a lot to do with Daddy," she added thoughtfully.

His head shot up. "What?"

"He said you didn't have what it takes to be a cutthroat defense attorney. He said you were too soft, and you've been trying to prove him wrong ever since."

Was he? Why did Peyton have to dredge up something Quinn didn't want to face—his father's disappointment in his choices? Malcolm Ross had said that he should consider political law, like his mother. Or teaching. That was Quinn's forte—winning people over with his charm and rhetoric. But the thought of politics and teaching bored him. So he'd gone against his father's wishes and pursued his own goals. With the help of Philip Rutherford Sr. Oh, God! Had his dad been right?

Was Peyton right?

"I like my job and I'm damn good at it," he said in his defense.

"Until now," his sister murmured.

"Yeah."

"You obviously feel something for this woman or you wouldn't be in such turmoil."

He stared at Peyton, his eyebrows knotted together.

"When you share a life-and-death situation with someone, you form a connection. Wyatt and I did." She looked at Quinn soberly. "Although it was more his death than mine. How dare he arrest me? I wanted to poke his eyes out with my fingernails. Now…" her voice grew dreamy "…I just want to love him for the rest of my life."

"How did you know it was love?" Quinn found himself asking.

"I couldn't stop thinking about him," she replied. "I didn't want him to think bad things about me. Up until then, I didn't care what people thought, as you well know. Whenever I was with him, I was out of my mind with happiness. The world didn't seem so hopeless and…"

Quinn held up a hand. "I get it."

"Do you?" She lifted an eyebrow.

He stood and flexed his shoulders. "I'm not sure I'll have those feelings for any woman."

"You certainly don't have them for Deidre. If you did, you'd be having this conversation with her instead of me."

Quinn never analyzed it much, but he had to admit he didn't have those feelings for Deidre.

"You'll be happy to know she and I are over," he announced.

"Oh, please." Peyton rolled her eyes. "How many times have I heard that?"

"My life's a mess at the moment, but I feel certain that's the last time you'll hear those words from me." He walked over and kissed her forehead. "I've got to go."

"Get that baby back to his mother as fast as you can."

"It's not that simple."

"If someone ever took J.W. from me, you would fight tooth and nail to get him back."

"I'm not Britt's attorney and I can't fight for her."

Peyton touched his face. "Oh, but I think you are fighting for her, and that's why you're feeling so torn."

On his way back to Austin, Quinn found his mind was in a tailspin. He had few options, but he planned to make the best decisions so he could live with himself. How he'd do that he wasn't sure. He would play this out to the bitter end and hope he had learned something from his father—to stand up for what he believed in. Quinn believed in justice. Britt losing her baby was not justice.

He might lose everything he'd worked for, but his conscience would be clear. And Britt would not view him as a bad person.

Somehow that was important to him.

Chapter Nine

Quinn fell into a restless sleep, but he woke up refreshed, and was in the office by eight. It was Saturday and, he had to admit, he worked a lot of Saturdays. He'd been told the Rutherford case was just a court appearance, a favor to a friend—simple, easy, no time drain on his own cases. To his surprise, more had been going on behind the scenes than he'd ever imagined. He didn't plan on getting caught in that trap again.

That's why he'd called Levi.

Quinn had to be prepared for whatever was thrown at him.

Levi breezed in, a coffee in each hand. He placed one in front of Quinn.

"Thanks." Quinn picked it up. "I was just fixing to make a cup."

"No problem." His colleague took a seat. "My engine doesn't run without coffee. And this is pure knock-your-socks-off black coffee. Nothing fancy in it."

"Didn't think so." Quinn took a sip.

"What's up?" Levi asked.

After several more sips, he placed the paper cup on his desk. "Just want to cross our t's and dot our i's on the Rutherford case."

"Like what?"

"I have a gut feeling the situation is going to get nasty."

"Figured that by the smear tactics."

"I want to be very sure what the men in the photos will say in four months."

Levi rested his elbows on his knees, staring at his coffee. "Mmm. You think with a little extra cash they might have something else to say?"

He nodded. "That's my fear."

Levi looked up. "Didn't I tell you I have your ass covered?"

Quinn frowned.

"I asked if they objected to being recorded, and all three said no. I have it all on tape—their praise of Ms. Davis and exactly what they were doing."

"Hot damn, Levi. It was my lucky day when you came to work for me."

The investigator twisted his cup. "I'm a little concerned, and keep in mind I'm with you one hundred percent…but who exactly are we working for?"

"That's where it gets a little sticky." Quinn picked up a pen and twirled it between his fingers. "I guess I should be honest with you."

"Aren't you always?"

"Lately, the line is getting blurred." But it was good to know his friend had this much faith in him. Quinn told him everything, from the creek flooding to the hearing, to everything he suspected.

"You feel Mr. Rutherford brought you in for the big showdown in four months?"

"I'm almost certain of it."

"Resign from the case."

"Then they'll bring in someone to really do a hatchet job on Ms. Davis."

"And that's got you?"

"Yes," Quinn admitted.

Levi stood and threw his cup in the trash can by the desk. "What do you want me to do?"

"Get those phone calls transcribed. I want every word on paper."

"You got it."

Quinn leaned back, tapping his pen on the desk. "Did you find out who's tailing Ms. Davis?"

Levi lifted an eyebrow. "Chester Bates. P.I. for the Rutherford firm, but I'm betting you already knew that."

"Just a suspicion. But I thought Phil would hire someone outside the firm."

"Why? Let Daddy-Big-Bucks pay for it." His friend stared at him. "I have a feeling you have something up your sleeve."

"I don't like being manipulated. Philip Sr. thinks I'll do anything he asks. But I draw the line at taking a baby from his mother."

"The baby is already with his father."

"Only briefly. I don't intend for it to stay that way."

"Crossing the Rutherfords will cost you—big. Are you prepared for that?"

Quinn ran a hand through his hair. "Yes."

Levi shook his head. "Never thought I'd see this day. The man with his focus on his career is risking it all for a woman he barely knows."

Throwing his pen on the desk, Quinn clasped his hands behind his head. "Are you with me?"

"Hell, yeah," Levi replied without pausing. "I love taking down a man like Rutherford."

"What if my plan backfires and I'm the one who's taken down?" Quinn had to think about that possibility.

"I'll give you a job on my ranch, minimum wage. Can you cowboy?"

Quinn laughed, a robust sound that released the tension inside him. He leaned forward. "I can wear boots and a Stetson as well as any man."

Levi's lips twitched. "That's not what I had in mind."

"Didn't think so."

"Like I said, I have your back. Just let me know what you need, and consider it done. I'll get the calls transcribed." Levi headed for the door and then stopped. "Need anything else on the Bailey or Morris cases?"

"No. Thanks for all your work."

"Call if you need anything." With that, Levi was gone.

Quinn settled in for the day. As he worked, the Rutherford case lingered at the back of his mind like an itch that needed scratching. Yes, he was risking it all for a woman he barely knew.

But he'd saved her life.

He knew her.

He knew Britt.

STEVE ARRIVED AND THEY worked on the Bailey and Morris cases, which were coming up at the end of November. Quinn was meeting with the D.A. on Wednesday and he had the first one hammered out to his liking. He just had to hone his argument a little more.

The Morris case worried him. Kathy Morris was a twenty-four-year-old mother of three who'd shot her husband in the back while he was eating supper. The D.A. was going for premeditated murder, and Quinn had his work cut out disproving that.

He let Steve go midafternoon. Since Steve had a girlfriend, Quinn knew he probably had a date. He'd almost forgotten that feeling of being young and full of energy. But it came in clearly when he thought of Britt.

Looking out his window, he could glimpse the capitol building, and in the distance and over the treetops loomed the University of Texas, his alma mater. He'd wanted to go to Harvard, Yale or Princeton, but his father had persuaded him to stick to his roots, his home state. Quinn had, and he'd never regretted that. But somewhere in a corner of his mind shadowed by the exuberance of youth, he wondered if his father had influenced his decision.

Did Peyton know him better than he knew himself?

Sighing, he reached for his briefcase and went home.

THE BUZZ OF QUINN'S PHONE woke him at seven-thirty Sunday morning. He reached for it on his nightstand.

"Quinn, it's Gail. I have a problem."

He sat up straight. He'd talked to her last night to make sure she would arrive at the condo early, to give Phil time to leave.

"What is it?"

"I'm here and Mr. Rutherford is refusing to leave. He told me to get my ass out of his house."

Son of a bitch! Quinn should have known Phil was going to pull something. "I'll be right there."

"Do you want me to stay?"

"No. I'll handle it from here, and you still have tomorrow off."

"Oh, thanks."

Quinn grabbed jeans and a T-shirt and quickly yanked them on, his anger boiling over. If Phil thought he could manipulate him again, he had another thought coming. Quinn could also play this game. And ethics be damned.

Slipping on his loafers, he hurried downstairs to his

study and found Mona's number. She answered on the sixth ring.

"Mona, it's Quentin Ross."

"What? It's Sunday." Her voice was sleepy.

"I know, but there's a situation. I wanted you to be aware of what's happening, and to know that I have everything under control."

"What are you talking about?"

"Phil is refusing to leave the condo, but I'm on my way to sort it out."

"Like hell. I'll meet you there."

Quinn hung up, a grin on his face. If he knew Mona Tibbs, she'd more than show up. And he was counting on that.

His first step over the line.

Since it was Sunday, the traffic was light. He made it to Phil's place in fifteen minutes. Britt's ex lived in an exclusive area not far from downtown. The condos were two-story, with private driveways and garages, all beautifully landscaped.

As Quinn got out of his car, Mona drove up with a police car behind her. She came with fire in her eyes, just as he'd planned. Thank God Britt wasn't here yet.

Quinn met her at the door. Mona wore a coat over her nightgown, he suspected. Her hair was pulled back into a short ponytail and her face was free of makeup. She'd left in a rush.

"What are you trying to pull, Ross?" she asked, poking the doorbell.

"I didn't know he was going to do this."

"Yeah, right." She held up some papers. "I have the judge's order in my hand and an officer here to make sure Phil Rutherford obeys it."

The door swung open and Phil stood there in his pajama bottoms. "What the…"

"May I speak to my client first?" Quinn asked.

"You have five minutes. I want him out before Britt arrives."

Quinn stepped inside and slammed the door. "What the hell do you think you're doing?"

"Whatever the hell I please. I'm not leaving my house on a Sunday."

"The judge says otherwise, so get your things and get out."

Phil's eyes darkened. "I'm ordering you to get rid of those people outside. I want them gone before Roslyn gets here. You got it?"

Quinn moved closer to him, his voice low and threatening. "I may be your lawyer, but I'm not breaking the law for you. You get dressed and get out, or that cop in the yard will take you away. Legally."

"You bastard. I should fire you."

"Go ahead."

The two men faced each other. They were the same height, and basically the same build. One was blatantly obnoxious. The other was pissed off.

"You'd like that, wouldn't you?" Phil sneered.

"Yes. I don't appreciate being dragged into this mess— your mess. If you feel anything for Roslyn Davis, you'll give her back her child and let her see you're a better man than she ever thought you were."

"Feel anything for Roslyn?" Phil laughed, a sound that was jarring. "I just want her to beg, and she will the day I take Dillon for good."

For good. That was the first time those words had been spoken, and Quinn wondered if Phil even realized what he'd said. For now he let it pass. He was more focused on the man's need for revenge.

He studied Phil's sinister expression. "Then why do you want her back? Why are you here waiting to see her?"

"Because this time—" he poked a finger into his chest "—I'll be the one walking away with everything she loves. I want her to know who's in control."

"Phil, I advise you to get some counseling, because you desperately need it. This is not normal behavior."

"She's trash, Quinn. That's all she is, and not worth your concern."

Quinn drew a long breath and curled his hands into fists to keep from striking the man.

"I've changed my mind," Phil said suddenly. "I'd rather not see the bitch."

Quinn nodded. "Wise decision. Get dressed as fast as you can and go out through the garage."

Phil walked away without responding.

Quinn went to the front door and opened it. "He's getting dressed. It'll take a few minutes."

"Then everything's okay here, sir?" the officer asked.

"Yes," Quinn replied, and noticed Britt was standing to Mona's right, looking worried. He forced himself to glance away.

"I'd rather you stay until Mr. Rutherford is off the premises," Mona told the officer.

A screech of tires burning against the pavement echoed through the quiet morning. Phil's Maserati whizzed by.

"He's gone," Quinn said, and opened the door wider. Dillon's cries filled the air.

Britt charged forward and ran toward the stairs. "Mommy's coming," she called.

Mona folded her arms across her breasts. "I take it, Mr. Ross, this won't happen again?"

"I'll do my best."

"I'll be going," the officer interjected.

"Thank you so much." Mona smiled at him. As the officer walked away, she turned to Quinn. "I don't know what your agenda is, Mr. Ross, but…"

"My agenda is justice."

She eyed him strangely. "I've heard that about you. I'm still trying to figure out why you called me."

"Justice, Ms. Tibbs."

"Yeah, right." Clearly, she didn't believe him. "I'm going home to my husband and kids. Britt knows to call me if anything goes wrong."

Quinn closed the door and went inside, shrugging out of his leather jacket. He laid it over a chair and looked around. The condo was very contemporary—muted walls with accent pieces in black, silver and glass. He wondered if Britt had decorated the place. It didn't seem likely. He pictured her taste as something more homey and comfortable.

Her voice came from upstairs and he headed there, finding her in the nursery. Leaning over a crib, she was talking to the baby as she changed his diaper.

"How's Mommy's Dilly bear?" she said soothingly.

The boy waved his arms and kicked his feet in excitement, obviously glad to see her. Britt removed his sleeper and slipped knit pants over the diaper, then pulled a T-shirt with a duck in front over his head. Dillon held up his hands, wanting her to take him.

"In a minute." She leaned down and kissed his cheek. "I have to put your socks on. It's cold."

He twisted and turned, but she managed to get them on his feet, and then she lifted him out of the crib. "Ready for breakfast?" The boy bounced on her hip. "I know you want your bottle." She walked out, not sparing Quinn a glance.

He went to his car to get his laptop and briefcase, and settled on the sofa. He was here for the day and he had to keep busy. But his attention kept drifting to Britt's voice as she chatted to her son in the kitchen. This was her time and he didn't intrude.

Engrossed in his work, he was taken aback when the baby shot around the sofa. The kid was fast on all fours. At the coffee table, he pulled himself up, slapping his hands on the glass and bouncing on his feet. Innocent big brown eyes stared at Quinn. Dillon looked just like his mother, and Quinn felt a catch in his throat.

The toddler spied Quinn's papers on the table and side-stepped toward them.

"Oh, no, you don't." Britt swung him into her arms, and childish giggles echoed through the room.

She sank into a chair, cuddling her son. "I was cleaning the kitchen and he got away from me. He crawls so fast."

"I noticed." And Quinn noticed her. He'd thought she was beautiful before, but with her baby in her arms she was stunning. Her dark hair was in disarray around her shoulders, and with that sparkle in her eyes and the glow of her skin, he found it hard to breathe.

"Why are you here?" she asked.

Chapter Ten

Quinn was so absorbed in watching Dillon, it took him a moment to realize she was talking to him. He cleared his throat. "The judge ordered it."

"But why you, specifically? I'm sure you have employees who can handle this." Britt bounced Dillon up and down as she spoke.

"I do, but she got a little flustered when Phil refused to leave, so she called me. I'm staying in case he gets it in his head to come back. Sorry that's not to your liking."

"I'd prefer if we had very little contact." Britt had to for her own peace of mind. Quentin Ross was a temptation she didn't need. He looked so different today, more like the man who'd rescued her. He wore faded jeans, a long-sleeved T-shirt that molded his broad chest, and a glint in his eyes that made her very aware of every feminine need in her. His disheveled hair looked as if he'd just gotten out of bed.

"Phil made that impossible." He waved a hand toward his laptop. "I'll work. Just pretend I'm not here."

As if that was humanly possible. Her attention was drawn to him every other second—to his hands, which seemed too big for the laptop as he typed. To his blond hair, which fell across his forehead. And to the thrust of his jaw, covered with a growth of beard. He oozed testosterone and every vibe found a mark inside her, making her very aware of what was missing in her life.

Dillon rubbed his face against hers and her heart swelled. She had everything she needed in her arms. But she only had him for the day. If she thought about it, she'd become upset, so she didn't.

"Playtime." She carried Dillon to his room to gather toys and books, and went back to the living room. They sat together on the floor, and she placed his blocks in front of him. He loved to stack them. After Dillon grew tired, she read to him. He slapped at the pages if there was a dog or a horse, his favorite animals.

"Do you mind if I make a cup of coffee?" Quinn asked.

She looked up. "Of course not." He probably hadn't even had breakfast.

Dillon grew sleepy and Britt knew it was his lunchtime. As Quinn walked back with a cup in hand, she said, "I brought Dillon's lunch. I'm going to the car to get it." She placed blocks in front of Dillon. "Mommy will be right back."

"I'll watch him," Quinn offered.

"Thanks." She fished her keys out of her purse and hurried to the door. As soon as Dillon realized she was leaving, he fell to his hands and knees and shot after her, crying loudly. She swung him into her arms, trying to soothe him. "It's okay. Mommy's here." She couldn't say the words she wanted to—that she would never leave him. Her temper boiled but she banked it down.

"I'll get it," Quinn said.

"Thank you." She handed him her keys and rubbed Dillon's back. "It's a small ice chest on the passenger side."

In a few minutes Quinn was back and handed her the

chest. "Why did you bring his food? Isn't there something here for him to eat?"

"I like for him to have something fresh and not out of a jar. I made him mashed potatoes, finely chopped up chicken and green peas. He loves it."

She placed Dillon in his high chair and tied a bib around his neck. He slapped a hand on the tray, knowing what was coming. After she heated the food in the microwave, she fed it to him. He gobbled it up. Growing sleepy, he rubbed his eyes.

She looked up to see Quinn watching them. He held up his cup. "I was just getting a refill."

"It's time for his nap." She lifted Dillon out of the chair and washed his face and hands. "I'm going to change his diaper and give him a bottle. The kitchen's all yours."

With Dillon asleep, she went back into the living room. Quinn was working at his laptop, a coffee cup beside him. Onnie had made her a sandwich for lunch out of leftover roast beef from their Saturday lunch. Britt hated to eat in front of him, or alone in the kitchen.

It didn't take her long to make up her mind. She grabbed the chest, two forks and two napkins, and carried them to the coffee table. Sitting on the floor, she pulled out food from the ice chest. "How about lunch?"

He glanced at her. "I'm good. Thanks."

"Did you have breakfast?"

"No. I left in rather a hurry."

She unwrapped the sandwich and laid it on a napkin. "This sandwich is huge. Onnie doesn't know how to make anything small."

Glancing over at the sandwich, he asked, "What kind is it?"

"Roast beef on Onnie's homemade bread." Britt pointed.

"Just look at that. It's enormous. I'll never eat it all. You have to help." She dropped her voice to a cajoling tone.

He closed his laptop and slid to the floor. "Okay. You've convinced me."

"And we have coconut pie, fruit and water. How's that?"

"Sounds delicious." He picked up half of the cut sandwich.

They ate in silence, and Britt couldn't help thinking the same thing she'd thought before: why did he have to be one of the bad guys?

"This is delicious," he said around a mouthful of roast beef.

"Onnie's a great cook. You should taste her spaghetti and meatballs."

He picked up a slice of apple. "I don't think I'll ever get that chance."

"Probably not," she muttered. They were on opposite sides and there was no way they could ever be together.

Except in her mind.

And she hated herself for even thinking it.

They shared the coconut pie and she pushed the biggest piece to him, licking her lips. "You have to eat the rest. I can feel my hips spreading."

He studied her mouth, and his eyes darkened. A sizzle of awareness coiled through her.

"There's nothing wrong with your hips," he remarked.

She gathered the remains and carried them to the trash in the kitchen, needing to do something to ease the tension in her stomach. "I wasn't looking for a compliment," she called over her shoulder.

"It wasn't one," he called back. "It's the truth."

She put the lid on the ice chest and placed it by her purse, then resumed her seat on the floor. Neither said anything else. Quinn leaned against the sofa, his eyes on her.

"I am sorry for the way things turned out."

She brushed a crumb from her jeans. "Somehow I believe that."

"I had no idea you were the Britt I knew."

"It makes no difference now."

"I suppose not." His eyes held hers. "I'm really not a bad person."

"You just work for people who are."

"I owe a lot to Philip Sr. That's not an excuse. It's just how I got caught in this situation."

"Were you and Phil good friends?" She drew up her knees and watched his face. His wide brow was slightly furrowed as he thought before he spoke, which she imagined he also did in court.

"Just law students together. That's how I met his dad."

She frowned. "I'm not sure what Philip has to do with my son. He never showed any interest in him."

Quinn shrugged and she knew he wasn't going to tell her anything else. Looking around the apartment, he asked, "Did you decorate the condo?"

"No. It was decorated when I moved in." Unable to stop herself, she ran her hands up her arms. "I hate this place. There are so many bad memories here."

"There had to have been some good ones."

"Phil's cruelty obliterated them all."

"I'm sorry."

"Then make him give me back my son." She held his blue eyes, mentally willing him to agree.

A loud wail erupted and Britt jumped to her feet. Her baby was awake.

The rest of the afternoon went quickly, too quickly. She didn't know how she was going to leave Dillon. She held and kissed him, and he picked up on her distress and became fussy.

"This is hard," she said to Quinn.

A look crossed his face, an expression she hadn't seen before. This was hard for him, too. That had never crossed her mind and it threw her for a second.

"It's ten to five," he said, glancing at his watch. "You better go before Phil arrives."

A tear rolled from her eye as she pulled a package of Goldfish crackers from her purse. Handing them to Quinn, she said, "Give him some of these and it will keep him occupied for a while." She held Dillon tight and kissed him. "Mommy loves you, Dilly bear."

Quinn sat on the floor and fed Dillon crackers. "I'll take very good care of him," he promised.

Holding back tears, she quietly picked up her things and slipped out, running to her car.

The moment Dillon realized his mother wasn't in the room he crawled to the kitchen looking for her. Quinn followed. Dillon's bottom lip dropped and he started to cry.

Picking up the boy, Quinn tried to comfort him. "It's okay, buddy. You'll see her again real soon." Dillon cried that much louder.

Through the wails, Quinn heard the front door open. He carried the baby into the living room. A middle-aged woman with graying brown hair was removing her coat. When she saw them she immediately came and took Dillon. He went to her, but his dark, watery eyes kept searching the room.

"I'm Debi Carr, the nanny. I'll take care of this little one."

Quinn reached for his jacket. "Isn't Phil coming home?"

"He said he'd be out late tonight, but don't worry, Dillon will be fine. I have a room next to his."

Dillon seemed comfortable with the nanny, so Quinn gathered his laptop and briefcase, his anger once again getting the best of him. The whole point of the hearing was so Dillon would be with one of his parents, but that was just a blind for what was really going on. To take Dillon from the person who loved him. To make Britt pay. To hurt her.

Walking out the door, Quinn knew every risk he took was worth it. If it was the last thing he did as a lawyer, Britt would get her son back.

BRITT CRIED HERSELF TO sleep, but was up early to start job hunting. Through the night she'd made a decision. She'd been dealt a crippling blow and it had sidetracked her, but not anymore. She was fighting back. Phil and Quentin Ross were not going to get the best of her. After showering and dressing, she called Mona.

When Mona answered, Britt got right to the point. "I'm not happy with what happened yesterday. Do something to get this changed. I should be able to see my son in my own home—his home."

"I completely agree with you and I'm already on it. I plan to call the judge as soon as I'm in the office."

"Thank you, Mona. I just don't feel comfortable with Phil able to pop in anytime he pleases. Make sure the judge understands that."

"I'll make that very clear. I'll call when I hear something."

Britt spoke with her mother and grandmother, and then hit the streets looking for a job. Carin wanted to loan her money until Britt was back on her feet. Britt refused. She had to make it on her own.

Every place she went, from department stores to dress shops to secretarial agencies, she was told the same thing— they weren't hiring. Finally she tried the employment office. She'd take anything. She had to have an income to keep Dillon and to pay the rent.

MIDMORNING, QUINN GOT a call from Judge Norcutt's office. She wanted to see him at one. He had a full schedule, but it was about the Rutherford case, so he made time. Getting in touch with Phil was impossible. The man didn't answer his phone or return Quinn's calls.

Quinn was running late and arrived a little after one. Mona was already there. They didn't have time to talk before they were shown into the judge's chamber.

Evidently Judge Norcutt didn't have much time, either. She was at her desk going through some papers. She waved a hand. "Please have a seat. As I don't have a lot of time, I'll get right to it."

She glanced at Quinn. "I understand there was an incident at the Rutherford house yesterday."

He stood. "Yes, Your honor."

"Can you guarantee it won't happen again?"

Quinn didn't have to weigh his answer. He had to be honest. "No. I can't."

"Due to Mr. Rutherford's disregard of the law—" she scribbled her signature on a document "—I'm changing the order. Ms. Davis will be allowed to visit with her son in her home. Mr. Ross, your office will continue to oversee the visits. The nanny will deliver the boy and pick him up at the designated times." The judge looked at him again. "Mr. Rutherford is to follow the order, Mr. Ross, and I trust you will see that he does."

"I'll do my best."

Out in the hall, he said to Mona, "I'm impressed."

"Thanks, and thanks for not throwing a wrench into the works. But I have to tell you this whole case stinks to high heaven." She turned and frowned at him. "And what the hell are you doing in family court, anyway, Ross?" She didn't give him a chance to answer. "It really ticks me off that the Rutherfords are using a high profile lawyer with a reputation for winning. That stinks, too."

"I'm glad you recognized that." He suppressed a grin.

She gave him a skeptical look before walking off down the hall, her heels clicking on the tiled floor.

Yes. He was very glad she'd recognized that. And he was glad Britt had a lawyer who was fighting for her. She needed one. But Britt had her own strength. She wasn't falling apart, just as she hadn't in the storm. From the start Quinn knew Britt was strong, and she'd need all that strength in the days ahead.

But in the words of Levi, Quinn had her back.

BY THE END OF THE DAY Britt realized that finding a job was going to be almost impossible. But she wasn't giving up. The next morning she hit more businesses, looking for work. She stopped at noon, had lunch and waited for Dillon.

She was ecstatic that Mona had gotten the ruling overturned. Dillon would now be home for a while. And he seemed to recognize that, smiling and crawling everywhere.

When a lady named Gail showed up, Britt was surprised at her reaction. She'd been expecting Quinn and was disappointed. How big a fool could she be? She had a knack for falling for the wrong men. Quentin Ross wasn't the man for her. He wasn't her hero.

But, oh, her heart wanted him to be.

Quinn wasn't there on Thursday, either.

Britt knew it was for the best, but she couldn't stop thinking about him or looking for him on Sunday. Gail arrived as usual.

It irked Britt that someone had to watch her while Dillon was with her. But Gail was very respectful of Britt's time with Dillon. She stayed out of the way, reading the paper, doing crossword puzzles or working on her laptop.

Britt had invited her mother and grandmother for lunch, because they wanted to see Dillon so desperately. Carin and Onnie cooked in her kitchen, and Dillon was happy, chattering and playing. It came to an end too soon. Dillon gave hugs and kisses as the two women left. Britt held on to him, bracing herself for when, once again, she'd have to let him go.

She was playing patty-cake with Dillon when her doorbell rang. It was too early for the nanny. Could it be Phil? A chill crawled across her skin.

Taking a deep breath, she walked toward the door.

Chapter Eleven

Holding Dillon, she glanced through the peephole and smiled.

Quinn.

Her heart fluttered with excitement. *Fool* rang through her head with vivid clarity, but she ignored that annoying little voice for now.

She opened the door. "Quinn, what are you doing here?"

In jeans and a leather jacket, he looked rugged, handsome and bad. Bad for her.

"I came so Gail could leave early." He walked inside. "I meant to get here earlier but I got sidetracked at my sister's."

"Oh, thank you, Mr. Ross." Gail gathered her things and was gone.

Quinn followed Britt into the living room. She sat on the carpet with Dillon and Quinn took a seat on the sofa.

"It's really annoying to have someone here to watch me," she told him.

"Sorry, it's the judge's ruling," he replied, removing his jacket. "Other than that how's it going?"

"Okay. Mom and Onnie came today and Dillon was so glad to see them." Dillon crawled to his toys on the floor and picked up a small NERF ball and threw it to her. It landed at her feet. She threw it back to him.

"How are you?" Quinn's eyes held hers and she found it hard to look away. How did he do that—trigger all her feminine emotions with just a glance?

"I'm better. I'm not so angry."

"Does that mean you're not so angry at me anymore?"

Instead of answering, she replied, "Mona said you didn't throw up any roadblocks at the meeting with the judge. I'm grateful for that—grateful to have Dillon home."

"That's where he should be."

She stared at him. "You're an enigma, Quentin Ross. I never know when you're serious."

Dillon threw the ball again and it landed on the coffee table in front of Quinn. He picked it up and held it out to the toddler. "You want it? Come get it."

Dillon glanced at Britt and then at Quinn. Clearly, he was undecided whether to trust this strange man. *Yes, you can* soared through Britt's mind like words from a well-loved hymn. After all that had happened, she still trusted Quinn.

And she trusted him with Dillon.

She was either the biggest fool who had ever lived or she was a romantic to the core who believed in love. As she let the thought simmer in her head she had to admit a hard truth. She had feelings for Quinn.

But they could never go anywhere.

Dillon shot across the floor and reached with one hand to get the ball. Sitting back on his butt, he chewed on it, his eyes on Quinn. Then he crawled over and handed Quinn the ball. In a second he took it back. They did this over and over, and Britt was amazed at Quinn's patience. Finally, Quinn threw it across the room. Dillon squealed and crawled after it, retrieving the ball and carrying it back to Quinn. It was plain to see that Quinn had a rapport with kids.

The doorbell interrupted them.

Britt rose to her feet. "Oh, my. I forgot the time. It has to be the nanny."

"I'll get the door," Quinn offered, "while you get Dillon ready."

Britt changed Dillon's diaper and bundled him in his coat. "Debi's here," she said to him, trying to prepare him for what was going to happen. "You like Debi." In the living room she kissed him. "Mommy will see you on Tuesday."

"I'll take very good care of him," Debi said as she took him. Dillon's bottom lip trembled and he whined.

Britt kissed him again. "Mommy loves you, Dilly bear."

Debi quickly left and Britt wrapped her arms around her waist. This didn't get any easier. She felt as if her heart were being ripped out each time. She brushed away an errant tear.

"Are you okay?"

She swung toward the voice, having forgotten that Quinn was still in the room. "You should go, too," she said instead of answering, and the tension was back. The tension that reminded her Quinn was Phil's lawyer.

Quinn noted the sadness on her face and his gut twisted. "I'd like to talk to you."

"About what?" She wiped away another tear.

"Your marriage to Phil."

"Why?" Her eyes narrowed. "So you can use it against me in court?"

"No. I'd just like to hear your side of the story."

"Why?" she asked again.

"Just trust me." For a moment he thought she was going

to tell him to go to hell, but the leeriness left her eyes and she walked into the living room and sat down.

Great. He wanted her to trust him again.

He resumed his seat on the sofa and looked around the apartment. This was Britt, from the comfy sofa and chair to the serene landscapes on the wall to the toys strewn around the room. It was comfortable. It was home.

Clearing his throat, he asked, "How long were you married to Phil?"

She curled up in the chair. "Barely six months."

"What happened?"

She tucked her dark hair behind her ears, her eyes troubled. "We argued a lot about my job. After we were married, he assumed I would quit. But I didn't. I couldn't see myself sitting in that big condo all day waiting for him to come home. The arguments escalated. We had a really bad one before I was scheduled to leave for four days. On the way to the airport my supervisor called. The flight had been canceled. At that moment I decided I couldn't keep up the constant arguing. I told my supervisor about my situation and quit my job. I felt better after I made that decision. I had to make my marriage work. I stopped for groceries, planning a special dinner for Phil."

She had a pained look on her face, as if she was reliving that time. "I'd just found out I was pregnant, and I was going to tell Phil that morning, but we'd argued instead. So I planned this big happy evening."

She stopped talking.

"What happened?" he coaxed.

"When I walked into the condo, I could hear music. Puzzled, I didn't even put the groceries down. I went straight up to the bedroom." She took a long breath. "Phil was there with a blonde in our bed. They were naked and wrapped around each other. Drug paraphernalia was on the nightstand. I was so shocked I dropped the groceries on the hardwood floor. The sound alerted them and Phil saw me. I ran, but he caught me at the door and said it was nothing, just something he did for stress."

The anguish in her voice weakened Quinn's defenses and he wanted to go to her, hold her and tell her all men weren't like that. He had to keep his distance, though. But he knew without a doubt the groceries on the floor were the ones in the photo—the picture Phil used to say Britt had trashed the condo.

"What happened next?"

"I left and filed for divorce the next day."

"Did you ever go back?"

"I went back to get my things when I knew Phil wasn't there, but he came home with the blonde as I was leaving. He wanted to talk and I said no way. He became angry and asked for my key, saying I couldn't take anything out of the apartment without his permission. I threw my clothes at him and left, and I haven't been back until last Sunday."

The clothes on the floor. The supposed second trashing. Phil was making up evidence, and if he thought Quinn would go into a courtroom with that kind of bogus proof he was highly mistaken. And so was Philip Sr.

Quinn cleared his throat. "And Phil let the divorce go through?"

"Not without a lot of threats. Then he found out about the baby and he repeatedly said he would make me pay." She sighed. "I guess he is."

"Do you have any feelings for Phil?" Somehow Quinn had to ask that question.

Her eyes flew to his. "Hatred. Disgust. Do those count?"

"I meant love."

She swung her feet to the floor. "I had my head in the

clouds and I believed that he really loved me. How naive could I be?"

"It's called trusting."

Her dark eyes flared. "I'm good at trusting the wrong men."

"Oh, that stings." Quinn held a hand to his chest.

"It should." A grin played on her lips and that light in her eyes was mesmerizing.

He cleared his throat again. "I better go." As he stood, he reached down and picked up the ball and handed it to her. His eyes holding hers, he added, "Trust me, Britt. Do you think you can do that?"

She stood, her eyes never leaving his. "You're Phil's attorney."

"Yes, I am."

"You're asking the impossible."

Unable to stop himself, he cupped her face and took her lips gently, tasting, cajoling. The scent of baby powder lingered on her skin and she tasted like the banana she'd fed Dillon. Quinn was drowning in the sweetness of her. Drawing circles on her cheeks with his thumbs, he traced her bottom lip with his tongue and she moaned, igniting a flame deep inside him. She opened her mouth and a new discovery, new emotions took over—powerful, explosive feelings that bound them closer than a flooding creek.

She drew back, her lips red and her eyes bright. "That might be an ethical violation."

"Yeah." He ran both hands through his hair. "I've been wanting to do that for a long time."

"You shouldn't. We shouldn't."

He reached for his jacket, just to do something with his hands besides touch her. "That's the trouble with emotions. They don't have a schedule. They just happen."

"Quinn…"

He touched her lips with his finger, not wanting to hear what she had to say because he knew it wasn't going to be in his favor. "Trust me, Britt. That's all I'm asking." Saying that, he made himself leave.

Trust me.

Britt stood with her fingers touching her mouth, remembering the feel of those male lips on hers—firm, yet soft and tantalizing, awakening feelings in her that she'd kept dormant. After being hurt so badly she had to be on guard, but Quinn demolished her well-established guard with just one knee-wobbling, heart-thumping kiss.

Trust me.

How could she do that?

In her heart she knew she already had.

THE NEXT MORNING PHIL stormed into Quinn's office before Quinn had finished his first cup of coffee.

"What the hell's going on?" Phil demanded.

Quinn waved Denise out the door. Evidently Phil had rushed past her. "What are you talking about?"

"The nanny now has to deliver the kid to Roslyn. How the hell did that happen?"

Quinn leaned back. "I called. My secretary phoned, but you never answered or returned the calls. How am I supposed to get in touch with you?"

Some of the anger oozed out of Phil. "I was busy. I figured you could handle whatever came up."

"I did. After your rude behavior, Ms. Tibbs asked the judge to reconsider her decision about where Ms. Davis could see her son. The judge asked if I could guarantee that you wouldn't do it again and I had to be honest, so she changed the ruling."

"You bastard."

Quinn's eyes zeroed in on Phil's red face. "Haven't you been home since Sunday before last?"

"Of course I have," Phil snapped.

But he paused, and that bothered Quinn. Was the man out doing drugs? Was Dillon in any danger?

"Then why the outrage now?"

"I've been working on a case and this is my first chance to get here. It just pisses me off that I have to pay a nanny to carry my son to his mother and pick him up."

Quinn leaned forward, his forearms on the desk. "Well, it pisses me off that one of my staff has to work on Sunday. That means I'm a person short on Monday and a half a day on Tuesdays and Thursdays. This whole thing is ridiculous and needs to be changed. Don't you agree?"

"Yeah, but that's the judge's ruling."

Quinn had Phil's attention and he was going to milk it for all it was worth. "I was thinking of a tracking device for Ms. Davis so we'll know where she is at all times. That would free up my people."

Phil's eyes lit up. "I like that. If she's tracked at all times, she won't be able to flee the States with Dillon, and I can pull my P.I. off her."

"Why do you have a P.I. watching her?"

"I want to know who she's seeing, when and where. But it's proved to be throwing money down the drain."

"Then get rid of him."

Phil pointed a finger at him. "You make sure she doesn't leave Austin."

Quinn nodded. "You'll still have to pay for the nanny."

"It'll be worth it. In three months Roslyn will fold like a greenhorn poker player and everything will go my way."

You sorry bastard.

Phil pointed his finger again and Quinn wanted to slap

him in the face. "Daddy's not going to be pleased at this turn of events."

"Daddy knows where to find me."

"Don't push him, Quinn," Phil threatened. "You'll regret it."

Quinn watched him leave with a steely eyed gaze. *It's only beginning, old friend.*

He touched a button on his phone. "Denise, tell Levi I want to see him as soon as possible."

A lot of things were going to change, and the action started now.

ON TUESDAY MORNING Quinn met Mona in the judge's chamber once again.

"What's this about?" Mona asked. "I just got a call to be here."

Judge Norcutt came in, preventing him from answering. Not that he planned to, anyway.

The judge sat down and adjusted her glasses. "I'm getting tired of rescheduling my day to suit you two. What is it, Mr. Ross?" She clearly was irritated.

He opened his briefcase, pulled out the item Levi had given him and placed it on the desk in front of her. "This is a tracking device, Your Honor."

"Why are you showing me this?" Her voice dropped from irritated to sub-zero infuriated.

"Your Honor, having a member of my staff off a whole day and two half days is putting a strain on my office. I need my staff at work, not babysitting."

"You're skating on thin ice, Mr. Ross."

"Hear me out, please. The device is a bracelet that will be locked on Ms. Davis's wrist. My P.I., Levi Coyote—you know Levi, don't you, Judge?"

"Yes. A fine cop and detective."

"Levi will have the control, and monitor Ms. Davis's whereabouts at all times. That should put your mind at ease about her fleeing with the boy."

The judge picked up the object. "It just looks like a nice bracelet."

"Trust me, it's more than that." And those words could ruin his whole career, yet he didn't retract them.

Judge Norcutt shot him a glance. "Is Mr. Rutherford on board with this?"

"Yes, Your Honor."

"Ms. Tibbs, how do you feel about this device?"

"I'll have to talk to my client."

"Fine. If Ms. Davis agrees, get it done, Mr. Ross. Otherwise the dictates of this court stand. And please stop bothering me."

"Thank you, Your Honor."

"Your Honor…" Ms. Tibbs spoke up. "I'd like the court to know that Ms. Davis has quit her job and is now searching for work in Austin to support her son."

Quinn was taken aback. Britt had quit her job. Why hadn't she said something? But then, why would she?

"I'll take that into consideration at the hearing," the judge replied.

"Pompous twit," Mona said out in the hall.

"Now, Ms. Tibbs…"

She turned on him. "What are you up to, Ross?"

"Don't look a gift horse in the mouth."

"Oh, I'm looking at a whole lot more and seeing things I'm not believing."

Quinn smiled. "Let me know what Ms. Davis says."

He strolled away, feeling victorious as he never had before. The line between right and wrong was so blurred now that he couldn't distinguish the difference if he tried. His whole career wobbled on that line.

He never strayed from his ethic of doing the right thing. It was his mantra. His goal. And he still believed he was doing so.

IN HIS CAR HE CALLED Levi.

"How did it go?" the P.I. asked.

"Like a charm. The judge bought it. We just have to wait and see how Ms. Davis takes it."

"You just put both our asses on the line."

"Have you ever been in jail, Levi?"

"Just booking people. But I'm not worried. I have a crackerjack lawyer."

Quinn laughed. "You might give me his number. I'll probably need him, too."

"Look in the mirror."

"Oh, him."

"Yeah."

Quinn negotiated a turn on to Congress Avenue. "I'm worried that Phil is still using. See what you can find out and hire someone else to watch his condo. I want to make sure the nanny is there at all times. Dillon's safety is the most important thing."

"I'm on it."

Quinn clicked off and wondered what Britt would say if she knew the bracelet was just that—a bracelet.

Chapter Twelve

"What? They want me to wear a tracking device?" Britt's blood pressure shot through the roof and all she could see was a red haze. "I'm not a criminal and they can't do that. I refuse to be treated this way."

"Calm down, Britt," Mona suggested, placing her briefcase on the sofa in Britt's apartment. "This was Quentin Ross's idea."

"What?" The raging blood drained from her face.

"I'm not sure what's going on, but it sounds like a good idea."

"How can you say that? I'm not wearing some bulky device like a hardened criminal."

"It's a bracelet. A very nice bracelet, as the judge said. To tell you the truth, I've never seen a tracking device like it."

She frowned. "A bracelet?"

"It's like jewelry, so no one will ever know the difference. And look at it this way—you'll have Dillon all to yourself. No one has to watch you."

"Oh." The situation was sounding better.

"So what do you say?"

"Mr. Ross did this?" That still puzzled her.

"Yes. Seems it's putting a strain on his office staff having to stop their work and come here. He says it's ridiculous and I have to agree."

"Is Phil going along with this?"

Mona nodded. "That's what Mr. Ross said."

Britt sat down, forcing her nerves to calm down so she could think. *Trust me.* Those two words kept running through her mind. After everything that had happened, trust didn't come easy. She weighed the pros and cons. The only thing that mattered was that she'd have Dillon to herself without someone watching over her shoulder. But wearing a tracking device still rankled her.

Trust me.

"What's your answer?" Mona asked.

She touched her lips. "Yes."

The lawyer picked up her briefcase. "I feel it's a good decision. I'll let Mr. Ross know."

"Thank you, Mona."

Britt sat there for a long time, hoping she'd done the right thing. And hoping she hadn't let her heart sway her, once again.

THE NEXT MORNING she was about to leave the apartment for another day of job hunting when her phone rang. She picked up.

"Britt, it's Quinn." Her heart soared at the familiar voice and she wanted to smack herself.

"Good morning."

"Are you going to be there awhile?"

"I was just leaving."

"It will only take a few minutes."

"What will?"

"My P.I., Levi Coyote, will put the bracelet on this morning. That is, if you have time."

"Okay."

"You sound hesitant."

"I don't understand why I can't be trusted not to leave the country with my child."

"Work with me here, not against me."

She gripped the receiver. "I never know what the hell you're talking about or whose side you're on half the time."

"Ah, Britt, just be patient." She could almost see the grin on his face.

"Okay." She gave in reluctantly. "I hope it's not going to take long. I have to find a job to support myself and my kid."

"Yeah. I heard you quit your job."

"I've been thinking about it for a while. Dillon needs me and I'll be here from now on. I just hate that it happened this way. And I hate that you're Phil's attorney."

There was a pause on the line. "It's a cruel twist of fate for sure."

"Mmm."

There was another pause, as if he was gauging his words. "Levi will be there in five minutes and it won't take long."

"Fine."

"Good luck job hunting."

"Yeah, right," she murmured, hanging up.

She took two steps and her doorbell rang. That was quick. The man must have been outside the whole time. She opened the door to a tall cowboy type in boots and a Stetson. He held a small box in his hand.

"Levi Coyote, ma'am." He tipped his hat, and she stepped aside, feeling as if the man was a leftover from an old Western.

"Come in." She closed the door behind him.

"This'll only take a minute," he said, opening the box

and pulling out a small silver bracelet. Undoing the clasp, he snapped it onto her left wrist.

She stared at it. The silver had an intricate pattern of x's and o's carved into it. When she twisted her wrist, the silver caught the light and glistened.

"This is it?"

"Yes, ma'am. You won't be able to undo it or to slip it off."

"How will you remove it?" She wasn't wearing it longer than necessary, even though it was rather nice, as Mona had said.

"I'll have to cut that tiny chain dangling from the clasp."

"Oh."

He pulled a cell phone from his jeans and punched in some numbers. Turning the screen so she could see it, he said, "This is how I'll keep track of you." He pointed to a red dot visible on the map displayed on the screen. "That's you. I can check your whereabouts at any time. Easy and simple."

"And annoying."

He shrugged. "You'll have to take that up with your attorney."

"Like that will move mountains."

He gave a lopsided grin, slipped the phone into his pocket and left.

Britt rotated her wrist, getting a feel for the bracelet. *Not bad,* she thought. She could handle this.

THE NEXT WEEK BRITT'S insurance company approved her claim for a new Camry. She was happy to have her own vehicle, but she began to despair of ever finding a job. Her savings were dwindling fast and she had to take whatever was offered. But there was nothing out there. The economy had caused many businesses to cut costs.

She thought stores would be hiring for the upcoming holidays, but they weren't. Just when she was weighing her options and thinking of moving back in with her mother, she got a call from a local McDonald's. She had no problem accepting. After all, beggars couldn't be choosers. It paid minimum wage but it was a job. The hours were six to one. Being just hired, she hated to make demands, so she explained about her days with her son. She wouldn't give those up. The manager, who looked as if he was still in high school, seemed sympathetic, and agreed to let her go at twelve forty-five on Tuesdays and Thursdays. Sunday was her day off.

She was just settling in at McDonald's, working with teenagers who made her feel old, and getting used to asking, "Do you want that supersized?" when the lady at the unemployment office called. She had an opening for a waitress at Threadgill's. Did Britt want the job?

She jumped at it, but again she had to explain about Dillon. They hired her to work six-hour shifts on Fridays, Saturdays, Mondays and Wednesdays.

It worked for Britt. She had two jobs, but she soon found that going on a few hours' sleep was getting to her. She could handle it, she told herself. The highlight of her existence was her time with Dillon.

She now took him out and about as she used to. They went to the park, which Dillon loved, and on Sundays they usually visited her mother and grandmother. It was almost normal. But it wasn't. Dillon wasn't with her at night. Debi put him to bed and got him up in the mornings. Dillon didn't have his mother. Britt worked tirelessly to make sure that when the hearing came, she would be able to take Dillon home.

She hadn't heard from Quinn since his P.I. had put the bracelet on her wrist. That was just as well. But she found she couldn't stop thinking about him. She'd gotten used to him checking on her.

She was probably always going to have a soft spot for Quentin Ross.

Some heroes were hard to resist.

QUINN WAS BUSY. HE'D plea-bargained in the Bailey case and was pleased with the result. Jerry would spend two years in a psychiatric ward and then be reevaluated. It was a good arrangement. Jerry would get the help he needed to deal with what had happened, and he had a chance at a life.

The Morris case was different. The D.A. refused to plea-bargain it out. The case was going to trial after Thanksgiving and Quinn had to be ready. Kathy Morris had three kids under the age of five. Quinn had gotten her out of jail, but he didn't know how long he could keep her with her kids. And the holidays were close—a hell of a time to go to jail and leave them.

He thought of Britt, as he so often did. How was she coping? Had she found work? He had to force himself not to go to her apartment, but his strength didn't last long. He wanted to see her. Grabbing his coat, he headed for his car.

As he passed the large Rutherford building on Congress Avenue, he thought of Phil. He hadn't heard from him or Philip Sr. But he knew it was only a lull before the storm.

Tailing Phil had been fruitless. Levi hadn't been able to find any evidence that Phil was still doing drugs. Levi was a damn good detective, and if Phil was, he would soon find the evidence. The good news was that Phil was home at nights where he should be.

As Quinn drove toward Britt's apartment, his cell rang. Pulling it out of his coat pocket, he glanced at the caller ID. Deidre.

He clicked on.

"Hi, Quinn. Are you still mad at me?" Sugary words wafted through the phone.

"I was never mad at you."

"Good. Let's do something tonight. I've missed you."

This was the part where he would usually say something about the new boyfriend. But he really didn't care anymore.

"Sorry. I'm busy."

"With what?"

He gripped the steering wheel. "I'm going to check on someone and then I'm heading home for a relaxing evening."

"That sounds boring."

"It doesn't to me. I've had a long day."

"Come on, Quinn. Let's go to the club and—"

"Deidre." He cut her off. "You said it was over and it really is over."

"You don't mean that."

"Yes, I do. Our merry-go-round relationship is truly over."

"You're being an ass."

"Goodbye, Deidre." He clicked off and drove on, knowing he'd let the relationship go on too long. He didn't worry about Deidre. She'd find someone else. She always did.

Ten minutes later he rang Britt's doorbell. And waited. He saw her car in the parking area, so she had to be here. Was she avoiding him?

Finally, he heard, "Who's there?"

"Quinn," he called.

She opened the door, tying a white terry-cloth bathrobe around her waist. Her dark hair was wet and disheveled. She'd just gotten out of the shower, he guessed.

Staring into her dark eyes, Quinn felt a tightness grip his abdomen, and the tiredness of the day seem to ebb away.

"How are you doing?" he asked, his voice husky to his own ears.

She opened the door wider and he stepped into the apartment. "You came all the way over here to ask me that?"

"It's on my way home, and since I left the office early tonight I thought I'd check."

She lifted an eyebrow. "You work this late?"

He removed his coat and sat on the sofa. "I have an important case coming up and it requires all my attention."

Her eyebrow lifted higher. "That wouldn't be…?"

"No," he assured her.

She tilted her head. "Why aren't you on a date with, hmm, what's her name?"

"Deidre," he told her. "We broke up."

"Really? I hope…"

"It had nothing to do with my being late for our date."

"Oh." Was that a pleased note in Britt's voice?

"How's the bracelet working?" he asked, to change the subject.

She sat in the chair and curled her bare feet beneath her. Raising her wrist, she said, "Fine. I hardly know it's there and I've gotten a couple of compliments on it."

"Really?"

"Yeah. The girls at McDonald's think it's oh so cool." She made a silly face as she said it.

"You're hanging out at McDonald's these days?"

She shrugged. "I kind of have to, since I work there."

"What?"

"There's nothing else out there and I have to work."

He'd had no idea, but she seemed fine with it.

"I work from six to one at McDonald's, and six-hour shifts at Threadgill's on the days I don't have Dillon, so I'm a little deprived of sleep. I was just going to bed when you rang the bell."

"I'm sorry." Quinn started to rise.

She waved him back down. "It's okay. I can pay my rent now." Her lips curved into a smile and he felt a jolt to his heart. Her hair was damp from the shower, her face bare of makeup, and yet she still managed to look gorgeous. She had a natural beauty that was hard to ignore.

"So...you're able to keep your days with Dillon?"

"You bet. I wouldn't take the jobs otherwise." She yawned, resting her head against the chair.

"I should go." Her tired face was about to do him in. He just wanted to gather her into his arms, hold her close and reassure her that her life would be back to normal soon. But he couldn't do that.

"Tell me about your case," she murmured, half-asleep.

He told her about Kathy Morris and the abuse she'd suffered. It wasn't long before Britt was sound asleep. Without thinking about it, he scooped her into his arms and carried her into the bedroom. The ecru sheet and peach comforter were pulled back. He laid her down and covered her.

"Quinn?" she whispered.

"Hmm?"

"Will the lady get to raise her kids?"

"I'm doing my best to see that she does." Gently, he tucked Britt's hair behind her ear and kissed her cheek.

And you, too. I'm doing everything I can so you can keep Dillon.

He watched her sleep for a moment, the classic lines of her face at peace. She made a wispy sound as she slept, her mouth slightly open. The urge to kiss those pink lips overtook him but he turned away. Reaching for the light switch, he paused. Dillon's empty crib was against one wall by a changing table and a toy box. They shared the room.

Every morning she saw that empty crib, and how that must hurt her. He hated his part in this whole custody debacle. His stomach churned with distaste and he glanced at her face. Yet she didn't seem to hate him.

He flipped off the light, quietly closed the door and let himself out.

All the way home he thought about how tired she was. How long could she continue going on so little sleep? He had to do something.

Pulling into his driveway, he saw the old Lincoln parked to the side. Harmon Withers, a colleague of his dad's, was walking from the front door. Quinn parked and went to meet him. Quinn had called him about the books, so assumed that was the reason for the visit.

They shook hands. Quinn's father had been Harmon's mentor. Even though there was a large age gap the men had been close.

"Forgive my rudeness in not calling," Harmon said in his soft-spoken voice, "but I was returning home after a late evening at the university and thought about the books of Malcolm's that you mentioned. On the off chance you might be home, I stopped. I do hope it's not an inconvenience."

"No, no. Come on in." Quinn unlocked the door and they went through the large foyer into the library. Quinn pointed to two boxes on the hardwood floor. "Those are the books I was talking about. Some are in foreign languages. I know Dad would want them to go to good use."

Harmon knelt near the boxes, as eager as a child, and gently opened a couple of the books. "Oh, yes. These are rare. I will gladly give them a home." Harmon pushed himself to his feet, using the desk for stability.

In his sixties, he was neatly dressed as usual in a three-piece suit, tie and a matching pocket square in his breast pocket. His gray hair was cut short, and his glasses were perched on his nose.

"I'll carry these to your car," Quinn offered.

"Thank you, Quinn."

After the boxes were in the car, Harmon asked, "Were you working late, too?"

"Yes. I have a difficult case coming up."

Harmon patted Quinn's shoulder. "Even though Malcolm was proud of everything you did, he always said you didn't have the heart to be a defense attorney. My boy, you have proved him wrong. You've helped a lot of people." Harmon tapped his glasses. "You see, I follow your trials in the paper."

"Thank you," Quinn said, and to get off the subject he asked, "And what is a professor doing working so late?"

"Oh, don't ask." He waved a hand as he slid into his car. "My assistant is on maternity leave and isn't planning on returning. I can't find anything in that office, can't even locate some of my research papers. Plus, I have papers to grade, which she puts into the computer. Now I have to do it. I don't have enough time." He shook his head in frustration. "Thanks again, Quinn." The door closed and Quinn waved goodbye.

Then it hit him. He knocked on the window before the professor could back out. The window slid down and Harmon squinted at him.

"Are you looking for someone else?"

"Yes, but I'm picky."

"I might know someone."

Harmon frowned. "She's not a ditzy blonde, is she?"

Did Quinn have a reputation for dating ditzy blondes? That stung a little, but he brushed it off.

"She actually has dark hair and is very pleasant. She's going through a bitter divorce and needs a job."

"Oh." The frown reappeared. "I don't want to get involved."

"I'll vouch for her."

"Well…" Harmon reached into his pocket. "Give her my card and I'll interview her, but I'm not promising anything."

"Thank you, Harmon."

The man drove away with his treasures and Quinn went to his car and retrieved his briefcase. Walking into his study, he remembered Harmon's words: *Your father didn't believe you had the heart to be a defense attorney.* He sighed, sinking into his chair.

"You were right," he said to the room that permeated Malcolm Ross. The abuse and the violence were getting to him. It was hard to find a measure of happiness for himself when he dealt with it every day. Maybe his career choice all those years ago had been wrong. Was he better suited to teaching law, as his father had believed, instead of practicing it?

Quinn removed his coat and felt the loneliness of the house. At Britt's he'd felt at home. But it wasn't the apartment that made him feel that way. It was her.

She made him feel at home.

Chapter Thirteen

"Quinn."

Britt woke up calling his name. She stirred, and a warm feeling suffused her whole body. Touching her cheek, she sighed, and then sat bolt upright.

The room was in darkness, but she felt Quinn's presence for some reason. Then she remembered last night and them talking about his case. However, she didn't remember him leaving.

The alarm shrilled through the apartment. Five-fifteen. Time to get ready for work.

She crawled from beneath the covers and flipped on the light, realizing for the first time that she was still in her robe. How? She tried to remember and couldn't. She had no recollection of going to bed. Had Quinn put her there?

Her hand went to her cheek again, which seemed to be extra sensitive this morning. Oh! His touch. His kiss. Her body remembered. And she'd slept through it. Damn! She must have been really tired.

The alarm buzzed again. She didn't have time to daydream. Slapping the off button, she gazed at the empty crib. That familiar ache inside her blossomed and she hurried to the bathroom. Dillon would be back in his bed soon, she promised herself.

She was rushing to the door when the bell rang. She

paused. Who was at her apartment this early? Tentatively, she checked—and realized she was spending a lot of her time looking at Quentin Ross through a peephole.

Slowly, she opened the door. He leaned on the doorjamb with a lazy grin, and every feminine sensory receptor she had came to full attention. He was so handsome in a dark, two-piece suit and long winter coat. His blond hair curled into the collar. His blue eyes twinkled.

"Morning, ma'am." His voice was low, infectious and any thought of resisting his charm went south.

"I—I'm on my way to work."

He handed her a business card. "This guy is a history professor at the university. He's looking for an assistant. Decent hours, good wages and benefits. If you're interested, give him a call."

Feeling like poor helpless Britt who couldn't find a decent job got to her. Even Quinn's charm couldn't wipe away that feeling.

"I can find my own job, thank you."

His eyebrow shot up. "A little touchy, aren't you?"

"And you are Phil's attorney, so stop being nice to me. Stop…"

"Stop what?"

Stop making me love you. But she didn't say that. Her pride wouldn't let her. "Stop helping me."

"That might be impossible." He reached for her left hand and fingered the silver bracelet, then tucked the card into her palm. "Just think about it."

Warm sensations shot up her arm. She raised her eyes to his and wished she hadn't. Those same sensuous emotions were in his. She melted like butter under a heat lamp.

"Did you get a good night's rest?" he asked in a low voice.

"Yes." Her reply was barely audible.

He bent his head and kissed her lips lightly, briefly, blowing whatever defense she had against him out of the water.

"Think about the job." After one last glance, he strolled to his car.

She let out the breath she was holding, turned off the lights, locked the door and ran to her car with the card still in her hand. Tucking it into her purse, she smiled. She had no idea where she and Quinn were headed. Every time she put up her guard, he found a way to break through it. Mostly with just his voice, his kindness.

A man like that couldn't be all bad.

She wanted to believe that with all her heart.

WHEN BRITT FELL INTO BED at eleven o'clock that night she was exhausted. Threadgill's had had a small band playing, and the place was packed with college students and families, as well as singles looking for dates. She'd been hit on more times than a Vegas stripper and was getting good at the smiling brush-off.

The music was loud, the patrons louder. But everyone came for a good time and good food. Threadgill's had been an Austin tradition for over seventy-five years. Kenneth Threadgill was the first person to have a liquor license in the county. Back then musicians were paid with beer. Things had changed since the olden days, but Threadgill's was still a favorite musical venue. She worked in the south Austin restaurant, which was next door to the old great Armadillo World Headquarters. The walls were covered with memorabilia of famed musicians, from Count Basie to Willie Nelson and Waylon Jennings, who had played the 'Dillo in Austin's musical heyday.

Britt served so many chicken fried steaks with Threadgill's Texas margaritas that she lost track. But the tips were good and she loved the friendly environment.

The next morning she was back at McDonald's, and wondered how long she could keep up the pace. She revived for her afternoon with Dillon. That made it all worthwhile. At times, though, she found it hard to stay awake. After the nanny picked up Dillon, Britt fished the professor's business card out of her purse.

Decent hours. Oh, God, she'd love decent hours.

Before she could stop herself, she called Harmon Withers, and she made an appointment for Friday at two. That was her rest time between jobs, but that was the only way she could work it. Hopefully, it was a step in the right direction.

Britt liked Professor Withers. He was a soft-spoken man who made her feel at ease. He didn't ask a lot of questions and that surprised her. His main concern was that she could use a computer, file and do research. Another concern was he wanted her to work quietly and not burden him with endless chatter.

She promised she could do that, and he hired her on the spot. That was strange to her. She'd expected a thorough interview. Red flags went up. Did Quinn have something to do with this? *Of course,* was the immediate answer. Now her options were to accept or just walk out.

She would be beholden to Quinn. But she already was—he'd saved her life. She had to look at this realistically, though. With a better job she had the added ammunition she needed to fight Phil in court.

"The position is eight to five, Monday through Friday," the professor was saying.

It gave her the opportunity to explain about Dillon.

He looked up from the papers on his desk. "Mr. Ross your attorney?"

She swallowed. "No. He's my ex's attorney."

The professor blinked, clearly thrown. "Interesting and totally confusing."

"Does it make a difference?" she asked.

"Not to me, my dear. You start on Monday if you want the job."

"I do, and thank you." The decision was easy, after all.

"Just do the work—that's all I ask—and you can have Tuesday and Thursday afternoons off. But you might have to take work home."

"No problem. I'll see you on Monday."

Britt left, thinking there were a lot of nice people in the world and she was grateful for their help. She wouldn't let Professor Withers down. Just as she'd never let her son down again.

Her life took a turn for the better. She quit her job at McDonald's, but still helped out at Threadgill's at night. She was saving every dime she could so she'd be able to rent a bigger place. Dillon needed his own room.

She and the professor worked well together. He was a quaint, eccentric man who liked his privacy, and Britt made sure he had that, fielding calls and dealing with students who just had to talk to him. She didn't know a lot about ancient civilization but she was learning.

Going to work at the university was a little different than McDonald's. She enjoyed wearing nice clothes, and the campus was beautiful with its gnarled oaks and historic buildings, which were overshadowed by the 307 foot UT tower. If the weather wasn't bad, she loved to sit under one of the big oaks and watch the students with their backpacks, laptops and cells phones, full of life and energy, with their whole lives ahead of them. She'd once been like that.

Then she'd met Phil Rutherford.

And she felt old and used up.

Until she thought about Quinn.

He made her feel young and alive again. She wanted to call and tell him about the job and thank him. But she hesitated. She had to do this on her own without any more favors from him. Every time he saw her she knew he was putting his job on the line. And she couldn't get involved with a man who was working for Phil.

But she couldn't change the fact that she already was. How were they going to fix their messed up lives?

QUINN WAS WORKING LATE again. It was the Wednesday before Thanksgiving. Jury selection for the Morris case started on Monday, so he was going to have a short weekend. Peyton had already informed him that he was expected for dinner on Thursday. His mother and her husband would be there, too. A family Thanksgiving, Peyton had said.

He eased back in his chair, thinking of Britt. She'd have Dillon for part of the day and he knew she was happy about that. Staring at his cell phone on his desk, he thought of calling her. She'd taken the job with Harmon and he wondered how she was doing. As he reached for his cell, Steve walked in.

"I can't find any precedent you can use in the Morris case. Damn! Why did she have to shoot him in the back?"

"When you're that afraid, logic is not a strong suit. I have to hope we get an understanding jury."

"It sucks, having her trial right before Christmas. If she's convicted, those kids will go into foster care."

"Well, thanks for the vote of confidence."

"Sorry." Steve's face turned a slight pink. "You know what I mean, though. This case is a bitch. But if anyone can get her off, you can."

Quinn waved a hand toward the door. "Go spend the holiday with your family."

"I'm staying to watch the UT and Aggie game with my brothers, but I'll be back in town on Saturday. If you need anything, just call."

"I will. And happy Thanksgiving."

"You, too." Steve frowned. "You're not going to work through the holiday, are you?"

"No. I have orders to be at my sister's."

Steve nodded and walked out.

Quinn would love to spend Thanksgiving with Britt and Dillon, but he knew that was impossible. He wasn't a member of her family. He was the man who'd taken her child from her. That still burned like raw acid in his gut.

Suddenly a shuffling noise came from the outer office and then he heard low voices. It wasn't Steve. *It couldn't be*.... He hurried around his desk and through the door, and there they were, Bonnie and Clyde. What were they up to now?

"Are you sure this is it, Ona?" Enzo asked. "It doesn't look the same."

"You don't remember anything, Enzo. Of course this is it. Now let's find Mr. Hotshot."

"Are you two vampires who only come out at night?" Quinn asked, walking into the reception area.

"What he say?" Enzo asked with a giant-size frown.

"He said you're a vampire," Ona replied.

"What's that?"

"Think Dracula," Ona told him.

Enzo's frown welded into his wrinkled forehead. Clearly, he didn't get it. Tonight he wore a baseball cap with the University of Texas logo on it, a heavy coat and pants two sizes too big for him. And he leaned heavily on a cane.

Ona wore a bright red knitted hat, a long gray coat and support shoes. In her hand was a large brown paper bag.

"Aren't you two grounded?" he asked.

"We've come to get my gun," Enzo said. "I had it since the war and I want it back."

"Sorry. Mrs. Davis told me to throw it away." It was still in Quinn's safe, but no way was he giving it to Enzo.

"What? She had no right. That's my gun." Enzo sank into a chair in front of Denise's desk. "Did you get any beer?"

Ona grunted. "He has the attention span of a child. I brought you something." She held up the paper bag.

Quinn eyed it warily. "Is that a bomb?"

Ona laughed, a real laugh, and Quinn knew underneath her hellfire and fury she had a sense of humor. "Hear that, Enzo? We never thought of a bomb."

"Yeah. Could have blown up the whole place, except I don't know how to make a bomb."

"Me, neither, but it's a hell of an idea."

"You know they lock people up for saying things like that." Quinn knew they were harmless, and he wondered if they even realized the consequences of their actions.

"Yeah. Go figure." She raised the bag again. "I made you a chocolate pie for saving my granddaughter's life."

"Ona makes good pies." Enzo bobbed his head.

Quinn took the bag. "So I'm forgiven?"

"Hell, no," Ona was quick to say. "But one good deed deserves another."

Quinn didn't think he was, but he thought he'd ask.

"Did you get any beer?" Enzo asked again. Loudly.

Quinn looked at the old man. "Are you even allowed to have beer?"

Enzo bristled. "Damn right. I can have anything I want.

I'm ninety-two and not on any medication. What do you think about that, hotshot?"

"I think it's great and I'm wondering why you don't buy your own beer."

"Because that sour-faced daughter of his won't give him any money," Ona said.

Enzo pointed his cane at her, his wrinkly face scrunched in anger. "Don't talk about Frances."

"I'll talk about that whiney, lazy, no good cheap-skate—"

"Time out," Quinn shouted, knowing this was turning into a full-blown argument. "How did you get here? And does Mrs. Davis know?"

"We came on the bus," Ona answered tartly. "Carin doesn't have a clue where we are. She's sitting with a neighbor's sick mother while they're out for the evening. It's their anniversary or something. Carin's always a sucker for someone in need. She brought me in earlier so I could spend the night with my Britt, and get up early to cook dinner tomorrow. Enzo wanted to get his gun and I wanted to bring you that pic." She pointed to the bag. "So here we are. Does that answer your nosy questions?"

He ignored the snarky attitude. "Does Britt know you're here?"

Ona shook her head. "Nope. We're over twenty-one and do whatever we please."

"I figured that one out on my own." He turned toward his office. "I'll get my coat and take you home."

"Did you get any beer?" Enzo asked again.

Quinn stopped in his tracks. "Enzo, I'll buy you beer on the way home. How does that sound?"

The wrinkles on the old man's face weaved into a smile. "Like the pearly gates are opening."

"Hallelujah," Ona said. "I drink beer, too."

Great, Quinn thought as he slipped into his coat. He was getting two old people drunk. Well, then maybe they would stop trying to kill him.

THIRTY MINUTES LATER they were in Enzo's room, the elderly man stretched back in his recliner, sucking on a Budweiser. Ona sat beside him in a chair, doing the same thing, her feet propped on a small coffee table. The TV blared full blast.

Quinn was about to leave when there was a knock at the door and Britt walked in. She stared at him, shock in her dark eyes, before her gaze swung to her grandmother, to Enzo and then back to him.

"Quinn, what are you doing here?"

"Your grandmother and Enzo paid me another visit and I brought them home."

"What did they do?"

"We didn't do nothing, my pretty." Ona took a big swallow of beer. "Enzo wanted his gun back and I baked Mr. Hotshot a pie for saving your life."

"You didn't…" Britt whispered to him.

"No. I didn't give him the gun," he whispered back.

"She baked you a pie?"

He nodded. "It's in my car. I wonder if it has strychnine in it?"

A smile curved her lips and his heart zoomed as if he'd stepped on a gas pedal.

"You look great," he said, his eyes lingering on her face.

She wrinkled her nose. "I smell like margaritas. I've been serving them all evening."

He leaned in closer and breathed deeply. "I love margaritas."

"Hey, hotshot, we need two more beers," Ona called.

Quinn groaned, but went to the compact refrigerator for the beer. Popping the tops, he handed the cans to them.

"See, Ona?" Enzo said, taking his. "He's not a bad man."

"Onnie, where did you get the beer?" Britt asked before he could say anything.

Ona thrust a thumb toward Quinn.

Britt gaped at him. "You bought my grandmother and my uncle beer?"

By the tone of her voice he surmised that wasn't a good thing.

"Yes," he replied. "Is there something wrong with that?"

"He's ninety-two. She's eighty-three. You figure it out."

"Just because they're older doesn't mean they can't still enjoy life."

She placed her hands on her hips. "Really? Enzo pees on himself if he has more than one beer and Onnie gets crazier than she already is."

"Oh, sorry." Quinn reached for his coat. "On that, I think I'll leave."

"Hey, hotshot," Ona shouted. "Why don't you come for dinner tomorrow? I always cook plenty."

"Thank you, Ona. I appreciate the invitation, but I'm visiting my family."

"Just as well," Ona muttered. "I'd probably try to poison you, anyway."

"Hell, no, Ona," Enzo yelled. "He buys us beer."

Quinn shrugged into his coat and his eyes caught Britt's. "I really am sorry."

She tucked a tendril of hair behind her ear. "It's okay. You're the only person I know who puts up with them, even after they tried to shoot you."

"I think they're all bark and no bite."

"Don't always count on that."

"I won't, believe me." He stared into her eyes. "Have a wonderful Thanksgiving."

She wrapped her arms around her waist. "I will. Dillon will be home for the afternoon."

"Good night," Quinn said to her alone, his voice low. Then he called to Ona and Enzo, "'Night."

"We need more beer," Enzo shouted.

Oh, God, what had he done? Quinn hurried to the fridge and removed the last two beers, stuffing them into his coat pocket.

"Hey…" Ona protested.

"Party's over."

At the door he paused, staring into Britt's eyes one more time. He needed the warmth he saw there to last him the rest of the weekend.

"Happy Thanksgiving," she murmured.

"You, too," he replied, walking out the door and wondering how happy it would be without her.

For the first time he realized how deep his feelings were for Britt and how much they'd grown since he'd rescued her from the flood. He didn't have to ask his sister how it felt to be in love.

He knew.

Chapter Fourteen

Peyton had outdone herself. The table was tastefully decorated with china, silver and crystal on a linen tablecloth
that had been in their family for years. His sister couldn't
boil water before she'd married Wyatt, so the turkey, dressing and all the trimmings were like a miracle in his eyes.
And the fact that it made Peyton happy was an even bigger
miracle.

Wyatt occupied the head of the table, while Garland,
Quinn and Peyton's stepfather, took the chair at the other
end. Maureen, their mother, and Mae, Wyatt's mother, sat
on one side, along with Jody, and he and Peyton were seated
across from them. J.W. was tethered in his high chair between Wyatt and Peyton.

Jody said the blessing and ended it with, "God bless
Elvis." No one batted an eye because they knew Jody's
Gramma Mae loved Elvis and it was always part of the
prayer in the Carson household.

Mae was as eccentric as Ona. They could even be
friends. Quinn shook his head, knowing he was getting
ahead of himself. He had no idea what the future held for
him and Britt. The next four weeks would be crucial. Philip
Sr. would make a move soon, and Quinn would have to
make the biggest decision of his life.

Peyton was puzzled by the chocolate pie he'd brought,

but everyone loved it, and he had to admit it was the best he'd ever eaten. Of course, he didn't tell Peyton, but her pumpkin pie didn't hold a candle to it. It was clear Ona was in a class all by herself in the cooking department. And a few other departments.

The conversation was lively, but Quinn's mind kept wandering to Britt. He kept glancing at his watch. Had Dillon arrived at Britt's? Was she happy?

"You're very distant today," his mother said. "Are you okay?"

"Sure." He wiped his mouth with a napkin. "I just have an important case coming up." He wasn't talking about the Morris case.

Peyton shook a finger at him. "No work today, big brother."

He made a face at her.

Maureen straightened her napkin in her lap. "I want all of you to come to Dallas for Christmas."

"Sorry, Mom," Peyton said. "We want the kids home for Christmas."

"Yeah," Jody added. "Santa won't be able to find us."

"Oh, sweetie," Maureen hastened to reassure her. "Santa will find you wherever you are."

Jody glanced at her mother and Peyton was quick to say, "Sorry, Mom, but you and Garland are welcome to come here and watch the kids open their gifts."

When Peyton was younger, she'd never stood up to their formidable mother. It did Quinn's heart good to see her now guarding her happiness like a lioness. He admired that.

And just like that, he realized he loved his family, but this wasn't where he wanted to be today. He laid his napkin beside his plate. "I hate to eat and run, but I have to get back to Austin."

"What?" The protest echoed from his sister and his mother.

He stood and kissed Peyton's cheek. "I really have to go," he whispered in her ear.

"Oh. Okay." She looked puzzled but didn't try to stop him.

He said his goodbyes, kissed Jody and J.W., and headed for the entry to get his coat. His mother followed him, as he knew she would. She was tenacious, one of the reasons she was so good in politics.

"Quinn, honey, do you have to go?"

"Yes." He slipped on his coat and looked into her concerned blue eyes. "I'm fine, really," he added. In that moment he knew his mother loved him and worried about him. She had done the best she could with her marriage to Quinn's father, and Quinn had no reason to harbor any resentment from his childhood. It only embittered him and he didn't want that. But he had to say something before he could completely let go of the resentment. He hadn't even known it was there until Britt had brought it up when they were waiting to be rescued.

He hugged his mother tightly and she hugged him back. "I forgive you," he murmured.

She went completely still, but didn't ask what he was forgiving her for. She knew. "I loved your father, but we grew so far apart we could never find our way back to what we once had."

"I know. Dad was hard to live with."

"I tried."

"I know," he said again. "And you don't have to explain anything to me."

She drew back and looked into his face. "What brought this on?"

"I'm finding out what real love is, and I don't want to hold any animosity in my heart that will tarnish it."

She held a hand to her breast. "Oh, Quinn."

He kissed her forehead. "I love you, Mom."

"Thank you, son." She paused, eyeing him. "Who…?"

Smiling, he opened the door and ran to his car. He wasn't answering that question.

Driving toward Austin, he could think of only one person.

Britt.

BRITT WAS HAVING A LATE lunch. Since Dillon didn't get there until one, she wanted him to play for a while before he ate. He was fussy today, wanting to be held. The separation was taking its toll on both of them.

She told her mother the whole story about what had happened last night, and Carin was aghast.

"What am I going to do with Mama?" she asked while Onnie was in the bathroom.

"Quinn said something about letting her enjoy life."

"But she tries to destroy more than enjoy, and what was Quinn thinking, buying them beer?"

"You know how Uncle Enzo is." Britt sliced an apple for fruit salad. "He's always asking for beer."

"But it's not allowed in the home." Carin shoved the sweet potatoes in the oven. "I'll probably be getting a call from Frances." She cocked her head. "Yeah. I hope Frances does call me. I'd like to know why she can't ever have her father for the holidays."

"He's happier with us," Britt commented. "He and Onnie grew up like sister and brother and they're kindred spirits."

Her mother groaned and Britt laughed.

TWO HOURS LATER THEY SAT at the kitchen table replenished from a meal mostly prepared by Onnie. Dillon had eaten and then started whining to get out of his chair. He fell asleep against Britt and she worried he was coming down with something. He wasn't his usual happy self.

"Every time I think about this custody thing I just get angry," Carin said, watching Dillon.

"We should have killed that bastard Phil instead of the hotshot attorney," Ona replied.

"Mama, I do not want to hear that kind of talk." Carin got up and carried dishes to the sink, her shoulders stiff.

Britt was about to go to her when the doorbell rang. She glanced at the clock. Three-thirty. It couldn't be the nanny. She walked to the door with Dillon cradled against her.

Looking through the peephole, she smiled and opened the door.

"Come in," she said to Quinn, taking in his lean physique, his dark slacks, white shirt and dress coat. A manly, fresh scent reached her and her stomach quivered. He was so tempting.

"Ona invited me and I thought I'd—"

"What are you doing here, Mr. Ross?" her mother asked over Britt's shoulder. Her angry Onnie-type voice was so unlike her.

"Mom…"

"I'd prefer if he wasn't here."

"Hey, Mr. Hotshot!" Onnie called from the kitchen. "Come on in. I'll make you a plate."

"Did you bring any beer?" Enzo asked.

"No, Enzo," Quinn answered, gingerly walking into the kitchen. "I'm not buying you any more beer. That got me in trouble."

"Sucker. The women got to you."

"See what he causes…"

Britt took her mother's arm and pulled her aside, still cradling Dillon in the other. "What's wrong with you? You're being rude."

"I'm just so afraid we're going to lose…" Her mother's voice cracked and she stopped.

Britt hugged her with her free arm. "Mom, let me handle this. Please."

"But he's…" Carin glanced at Quinn.

Dillon stirred against Britt and she thought it was time to get her mother's mind on something else. "Look. Dilly bear's awake."

Carin reached for her grandson and carried him into the living room. Dillon looked back at Britt, but didn't cry. She saw that Onnie was stuffing Quinn with pumpkin pie and whipped cream. Like her mother, Britt wondered what Quinn was doing here. But unlike Carin, she was happy to see him. She couldn't seem to get it through her head that she should hate him.

"They're fattening me up for something," Quinn said when he saw her. His voice was soothing and affable, washing away her doubts. "And I don't think it's for something good."

"You'll never know, hotshot." Onnie piled more whipped cream on the pie.

Her mother settled down and Dillon started playing with his toys, carrying the NERF ball to Quinn, as if he remembered. Football was on the TV and Britt sat on the floor with Dillon, and Quinn joined them. The toddler climbed all over him, slobbering on his clothes, and he didn't seem to mind. Her mother watched them closely. That didn't escape Britt.

Uncle Enzo fell asleep in a chair and Onnie snoozed on the sofa. The afternoon passed quickly. Soon Debi arrived, and Dillon clung to Britt. It made letting go that much harder. She told Debi to be sure to watch him because she felt he was coming down with something.

Her mother and grandmother packed up their things to go home. Quinn was in the living room with Enzo.

"Please come home with us," Carin begged Britt. "I hate for you to be here by yourself."

"I have to work at the restaurant tomorrow. I'll be fine."

Carin glanced toward the living room. "Why is he still here?"

"Give it a rest," Ona said, placing dishes in a bag. "There's more than one way to trap a weasel."

Carin blinked. "We're not trapping weasels."

"Oh, but we are, sweet daughter." Ona grabbed her purse. "Let's go. We have to take Enzo to the home."

"I'll take Enzo. It's on my way," Quinn said, and Britt wondered how long he'd been standing there and how much he'd heard.

"There's no need, Mr. Ross." Her mother's voice was as cold as she'd ever heard it.

"I'm going with Mr. Hotshot." Enzo fitted his baseball cap on his head and reached for his cane. "He might buy me beer."

Carin whirled toward Quinn. "Do not buy him any more beer."

Quinn nodded and glanced at Britt. She gave a tentative smile and suddenly knew why he had come today. He wanted to be with her as much as she wanted to be with him. And God help her, that just made their situation worse.

"Are we going by any strip clubs?" Enzo asked Quinn as they walked toward the door.

Her mother gasped.

"Sorry, Enzo," Quinn said. "No beer, no strip clubs."

"You're still more fun than Carin."

"Boy, he said a mouthful," Ona remarked.

"Don't start with me, Mama."

"Goodbye, my pretty." Onnie hugged Britt. "Let's go, Carin. Maybe we can stop for a beer so you can loosen up a bit."

The words hit a nerve. Her mother's face became pinched and Britt thought she was going to cry. Britt immediately went to her.

"Mom…it's okay. Onnie is teasing."

"I'm just so worried about you."

"Listen to me." Britt hugged her mother. "I'll be fine. I'll get through this, but I need you to be strong."

"Okay." Carin sniffed. "I love you, baby."

"I love you, too, Mom. I'll call tomorrow." She playfully shook a finger in her face. "And do not stop at any beer joints."

Carin laughed and the sound made Britt feel better. They would get through this—as a family.

THE APARTMENT WAS VERY quiet after everyone had gone. She checked the kitchen, but Onnie had made sure it was spotless. Britt picked up Dillon's toys and took a shower. It was too early to go to bed, so she decided to watch TV. It had been a while since she'd had any time to relax. She flipped through the channels and found nothing she liked. Curling up on the sofa, she promptly fell asleep.

The doorbell woke her.

She turned off the TV and stumbled toward the door, tying her robe tighter. Looking through the peephole, she was surprised to see Quinn again. Had something happened to Uncle Enzo? She quickly opened the door.

"What happened? What's wrong?"

Quinn stepped in and closed the door. "I forgot to do something."

"What?" she asked, completely baffled.

"This." He slipped his arms around her waist and pulled her to him. His eyes twinkled into hers as he took her lips. With a moan she leaned into him, soaking up the scent of the outdoors, the cold and him. It enveloped her, and thoughts of stopping never entered her mind.

As the kiss deepened, her arms slid up the sleeves of his coat to his neck. Her mouth opened, inviting him in to new discoveries, new heights of passion. The kiss went on until he trailed kisses from her mouth to her cheek, to her chin and to the warmth of her throat.

She arched her neck as every need in her came alive. At that moment the cold hard truth hit her and she pushed away. *He was Phil's lawyer.*

She flipped back her tangled hair. "We shouldn't do this."

"I know." Quinn took a long breath and she saw the desire in his hooded eyes, just as she'd seen before. She closed hers and blocked it out. *Tell him to go. Tell him to go.* But not one word left her mouth.

Nor did he make a move to leave.

"I can't get you out of my head," he said with a ragged sigh.

"Me neither," she admitted in a voice she didn't recognize.

He cupped her face with one hand and made circles on her cheek with his thumb. Coherent thoughts were impossible when he was touching her. Besides, she didn't want to think. She just wanted to feel.

She leaned her face into his palm, giving in to something stronger than herself. In that moment she knew she'd made a decision. He knew it, too.

. He swung her up in his arms and strolled into her bedroom, his warm, seductive lips taking hers in a slow, burning kiss that obliterated any lingering doubts. She slid from his embrace and pushed his coat from his shoulders.

"Are you sure?" he asked, his eyes a sleepy dark blue.

Nodding her head, she unbuttoned his shirt. When she touched his chest, he groaned, and in a matter of frenzied seconds their clothes were on the floor. He paused for a moment to stare at her, his eyes cloudy with need.

"God, you're so beautiful," he said in a husky voice as he pulled her naked body to him. His hands were gentle, coaxing, as they touched her back, her bottom. Every hard muscle of his magnificent frame pressed into her. She gasped at the sheer gratification. Turning, they fell backward onto the bed. He kissed her deeply and then his lips explored her breasts, her stomach and below.

Wispy sighs of pleasure left her throat and she reached for him, her hands massaging his strong shoulders and traveling through the swirls of blond chest hairs arrowing down to his groin. When she touched his hardness, he let out a long breath and pulled her to him, pressing every muscle into her once again.

Her senses throbbed, and they both knew they'd reached a point of no return. He took her lips and rolled her to her back. The kiss went on and on, and she opened her legs, needing more. With one sure thrust he was inside her. Her body accepted him gladly, willingly, as they joined in a primitive dance as old as time that bound them together closer than they had ever been.

She cried his name as waves of pleasure convulsed through her. A moment later he gasped and shuddered against her in release. They lay still as their sweat-bathed bodies enjoyed the aftermath.

Britt had made love before, but never like this, never

with all her heart and all her body. Finally, Quinn rolled to the side and gathered her against him. She drifted into sleep with her head on his chest, feeling at peace for the first time in a long time.

QUINN WATCHED HER SLEEP, brushing her dark hair from her face. He felt rejuvenated, alive. He now knew the difference between having sex and making love. The heart had to be involved totally and completely. From the moment he'd looked into her dark eyes he had probably known this day was coming. But he'd never dreamed it would be with this much intensity, this much emotion.

He didn't question the right or wrong of what had happened. Even though love words hadn't been spoken, they were there in every kiss, every touch.

Pulling her closer, he whispered, "I love you." And knew the days ahead would be a test of that love.

Chapter Fifteen

Quinn worried how Britt was going to feel when she woke up, but he needn't have. In the middle of the night she woke him with sweet kisses and they explored a new realm of lovemaking. Afterward they made turkey sandwiches. They were hungry from all the exercise.

Later, they sat on the sofa in the darkened living room, completely naked, sipping wine and talking about her job with Harmon, and other, inane things. He'd never felt a connection to any other person like he did with Britt. It had been that way from the start.

In the morning he reached for Britt, but she wasn't there. Fear shot through him and he sat up, glancing around. He relaxed as he saw her in the bathroom, putting up her hair.

Glancing at the clock on the nightstand, he saw it was after ten. What? He never slept this late, not even when working long hours on a trial.

"Where are you going?" he asked.

She applied lipstick. "To work."

"Oh." He wanted to ask her to skip work, but he didn't. Making her own way was important to her and he wouldn't interfere with that. "What time do you get off?"

She came out of the bathroom in tight jeans and a T-shirt that had Threadgill's written on it, her dark hair neatly pinned back. Her skin glowed and a need uncurled inside him.

"At six," she replied, putting her lipstick in her purse. Glancing at him, she asked, "Will you be here when I get back?"

"Do you want me to be?"

Her eyes held his. "Yes."

He grinned. "Then I'll be here."

She leaned over and kissed him. Holding her face, he deepened the kiss.

"You're not playing fair," she whispered against his lips.

He let her go with a disgruntled sound and she laughed. "You're insatiable."

"For you."

They stared at each for a long moment, both knowing they'd crossed a line last night that neither could undo. And they were comfortable with that.

BRITT LIVED IN A FAIRY TALE for three days. She rushed to work and then hurried home to be with Quinn. They made love and talked about their lives, sharing tidbits they hadn't revealed before. It felt right, natural, for them to be together. Spending time with him eased the ache inside her and she didn't miss Dillon so much.

Quinn worked on the Morris case while she was at the restaurant, and she thought about her own case, but didn't bring it up. Saturday night, though, after passionate, heated sex, Britt lay awake cradled in Quinn's arms. Her eyes caught the crib—the empty crib. And tonight she couldn't ignore it. When Quinn went to sleep, she slipped out and curled up in a chair.

She was in love with a man who had taken her child. And he was still Phil's attorney. Reality hit her. What was she doing? Once again she'd followed her heart without thinking. It could cost her more than she'd ever dreamed.

Quinn stirred and reached for her in the bed. Realizing she wasn't there, he sat up, brushing his hair from his forehead. The moon was bright, so he could see her sitting in the chair.

"What's wrong?" he asked.

"I saw the empty crib and…"

"Britt…" He made to come to her, but she held out her hands to stop him.

"No. I want to talk."

"Okay." He eased back on the bed.

She swallowed hard, saying the words she had to. "Please resign from the Rutherford case."

The silence in the room became deafening.

"I can't do that."

She felt a blow to her chest and had trouble breathing.

"Britt, trust me."

"You keep saying that, but I don't have my baby. He won't be home for Christmas or his birthday. I'm all out of trust."

"Britt." Quinn came toward her then, naked, the moonlight glistening off his long, lean body. But she held tight to her control. "I have other clients who depend on me, so I have to be careful how I handle the Rutherford situation. Trust me not to hurt you."

At the softness of his voice, she weakened. Her heart pulled her in one direction, her mind in the other. But Dillon had to be her top priority. She couldn't think about herself. "No." She got out of the chair and moved as far away from Quinn as she could. "I'm asking you again. If you feel anything for me, please resign from this case."

Their future hung between them. And it was all up to him.

He ran his hands through his tousled hair. "I can't. Just—"

"Get out," she shouted.

"Let me explain," he pleaded.

"Not unless it ends with you quitting the Rutherford case."

Grabbing his jeans, he slipped into them. Within a minute he was dressed, and strolled from the room.

When she heard the click of the front door, she curled up in the bed, her arms around Quinn's pillow, and cried loudly, the sobs coming from deep in her heart. She had gambled and lost. He didn't love her enough to give up his career. And she was aware that's what it came down to. The Rutherfords would ruin Quinn if he resigned. Just like they had ruined her life. Now she had to wonder how far they would go to take her child permanently.

And if Quinn would do their bidding.

QUINN STOOD OUTSIDE BRITT'S door, feeling pain like he'd never felt before. He'd hurt her and that was the last thing he'd wanted to do. Time was all he needed. Why couldn't she give him time?

Because her child's future was involved. He understood that. But he wanted her to trust him—trust him not to hurt her or Dillon. He could go back in there and force her to listen to him, but what would that accomplish? He couldn't give her any guarantees, and that's what she wanted. A guarantee for a future with her son.

And with him.

"Goodbye." He lightly touched her door before walking away.

QUINN THREW HIMSELF INTO the Morris case and tried to keep memories of Britt at bay. The jury was seated on the first day and they went to trial. He portrayed Kathy Morris as a woman who lived in fear. She'd suffered physical and mental abuse from her husband for years, but when he started beating the kids she'd snapped. She'd feared for her children's lives.

Through three days of grueling testimonies and cross-examinations, Quinn hung in there, trying to convince the jury that Kathy Morris did not belong in jail. The jury was finally sequestered, and Quinn waited. On Friday the verdict came in.

The jury was deadlocked.

The judge asked them to go back and see if they could reach a verdict. The foreman said it was useless. None of them were budging on their decision. Quinn was relieved. The state would now plea-bargain with him to avoid another trial. Kathy Morris would get the help she needed and she'd be home for Christmas with her kids.

Quinn had fought hard for the Morris case, with Britt and Dillon at the back of his mind. Why couldn't Britt trust him to do the same for her?

He returned to his office amid congratulations from his staff. Denise, however, kept rolling her eyes and nodding toward his door.

Shaking off her strange behavior, he strolled toward his office. The door was slightly ajar. He pushed it opened and stopped short.

Philip Sr. was sitting in a leather chair across from Quinn's desk.

Showdown!

Quinn shook the man's hand. Of medium height, Philip was dressed in a tailored suit, with his styled silver hair perfectly in place, as always. He was slick, suave and cunning. Quinn had to be on his toes.

"Congratulations," Philip said. "I believe you could get a cold-blooded murderer off."

"I wouldn't represent a cold-blooded murderer," Quinn replied, sliding into his chair.

"High ethics." Philip resumed his seat. "I admire that."

Quinn didn't feel that required an answer, so he waited for the proverbial shoe to drop. And felt it was coming with the force of a Peterbilt truck.

"I'm in town catching up on some details at my firm." Philip formed a steeple with his fingers. "And I wanted to touch base with you on Phil's case."

"What about it?" he asked in his best courtroom voice.

Philip glanced at Quinn over the tips of his fingers. "I want you to go after Ms. Davis. I want that child to stay with Phil—permanently."

Quinn leaned back, his hands resting on the arms of his chair. "On what grounds?"

"Wallis sent you plenty of grounds."

Quinn reached for the Rutherford folder on his desk and pulled out the photos Levi had blown up. "Are you talking about these?"

"Yes. She trashed his condo. She has a bad temper. Not to mention that she sleeps around. She's not fit to be a mother."

Quinn's jaw clenched. "I don't use evidence that other people have collected. I do my own investigation." He pointed to one photo. "In this one, food items are strewn on the floor. Nothing else is disturbed. I investigated further and found the groceries were what Ms. Davis bought to celebrate with Phil on the news of her pregnancy, and to tell him she was quitting her job. She dropped the bag when she found Phil in bed with another woman, doing drugs."

Philip rose to his feet in a slow, sure movement. "My son does not do drugs. If that bitch told you that, she's lying."

"Are you positive?" Quinn asked, his eyes never wavering from the older man's lethal gaze.

"How dare you question me."

Quinn stood, the tension in the room a tangible thing he could feel down to his bones. This was where he was supposed to fold like a frightened intern. He did just the opposite, and it wasn't as hard as he'd thought it would be. "I'm not arguing a case on fabricated evidence, and that's all Wallis has. No temper. No affairs. It's all false."

Philip's eyes narrowed. "I don't think you know who you're talking to."

Quinn stared straight at the man he had once thought could walk on water. "Yes, sir, I do, and my advice is to leave that child with his mother."

Philip slipped his hands into the pockets of his slacks with a sly grin. "That wouldn't be because you have a connection to Ms. Davis?"

Quinn tensed, but made certain nothing showed on his face.

"You see, I know you and Ms. Davis were rescued together from the Brushy Creek flooding."

"Is that why Wallis suddenly became ill and I got the call?"

"Thought it would be a nice touch for Ms. Davis." The chill in Philip's eyes got a few degrees colder as he pulled some snapshots from his pocket and laid them on the desk. Photos of Quinn and Britt kissing at her front door....

Son of a bitch!

"I'm always in control. Remember that."

Quinn raised his eyes to the older man's. "I never forget it."

"Good. We're clear then. File for permanent custody on new grounds."

Quinn took a sharp breath. "I told you I'm not arguing a case on fabricated evidence."

"Excuse me?" Philip bristled at his audacity.

"You heard me."

"You just signed your death warrant as a lawyer. I'll have you disbarred, and you'll never work again in this state or in this country. I hope she's worth it." He walked to the door. With his hand on the knob, Philip looked back. "I'll send a courier for all the files and anything else you have on the case. You're no longer the lawyer of record."

Quinn sank into his chair and let out an agonized sigh. Luckily, he'd gotten through his caseload before the holidays. No one was depending on him except clients scheduled for the New Year. To keep his license he now had to fight fire with fire.

He pushed a button on the phone. "Get Levi over here as soon as possible."

BRITT HAD TO STAY BUSY to keep from thinking about Quinn. He had to make a choice, and she knew it wasn't easy for him. It wasn't for her, either. Her broken heart was evidence of that. Some relationships weren't meant to happen, and she and Quinn would never be together. They were on opposites sides. He wasn't her hero. She'd accepted that.

Professor Withers made work a joy. When he learned she had two years of college, he encouraged her to continue her education. He said she could take a couple of classes and still keep her job. The more she thought about it the more she liked the idea. Elementary education had been her choice of major years ago, and it still was. She could work in the school system when Dillon was enrolled.

But first she had to make sure her son was returned to her. She had several meetings with Mona and told her she wanted Dillon either on Christmas Eve or Christmas Day. Mona made the request and it was denied. That was a devastating blow. She wouldn't see her son until after Christmas, but was determined not to let it get her down. Dillon wouldn't know the difference. Only she would.

She put up a tree in the living room just for Dillon, and bought his presents. Even the judge couldn't diminish the love in her heart. As she hung each ornament, she wished Quinn was here, just to hold her, to make the pain go away.

There was nothing so lonely as spending Christmas alone. She had her mother and Onnie, but she didn't have Dillon.

And she didn't have Quinn.

All she had to do was call him, but that would change nothing. He would still be Phil's attorney.

QUINN PACED IN HIS OFFICE and swung around as Levi entered. "Have you got anything?"

The P.I. shook his head. "Not a lot. Phil was gone from his condo three nights in the last two weeks. He's spending time with a woman named Jenna Lawson. She works in his office and she's stayed four nights at the condo."

"Nothing else?"

Levi shook his head.

"Come on, Levi. You're a better detective than that." Quinn sank into his chair. "The only way to get out of this mess and to get Dillon out of that house is to prove Phil is doing drugs. I know he is. Britt wouldn't lie."

"Maybe he's just a social user."

"Doesn't matter. Either way we need evidence." Quinn

tapped his fingers on the desk. "Where does he go with this Jenna woman?"

"Her apartment or his condo. That's it."

"Strange," Quinn mumbled, mostly to himself. "You'd think she'd want to go out and party or something."

"I thought the same thing."

Quinn tapped his fingers louder as he thought. "Do they take Dillon out?"

"No. He's always with the nanny."

Quinn touched the files on his desk. "I've been doing a lot of checking on Phil, but Philip has called in a lot of favors. No one's willing to talk or risk being blackballed in this town."

"Must be nice to have that much power."

"Yeah." Quinn stood. "I have a meeting with Judge Norcutt."

Levi pushed back his hat. "Is that necessary?"

"Yes. I want her to know what's going on."

"Don't burn all your bridges."

"I think I already have." Quinn reached for his coat. "Keep digging for something I can use. My office is closed until after the holidays, so I'll be able to help you. Between us we have to find the evidence we need."

Levi faced him. "Or you'll lose it all."

"That's about it." Quinn walked out, knowing none of it mattered except losing the woman who'd stolen his heart. She might not trust him, but he was risking everything to return Dillon to her.

JUDGE NORCUTT WAS WAITING for him in her office. "Make this short, Mr. Ross. I don't have a lot of time, since I'm clearing my schedule for the holidays."

"It's about the Rutherford case."

"It's the only case you have in my court, so that's a given."

Quinn looked right at her. "You made the wrong decision in that case. The boy should have stayed with his mother."

"Excuse me?" Her eyes flared behind her glasses. "You're skating very close to the edge, Mr. Ross. You're Rutherford's attorney, and you either retract those words or I'll file a complaint against you for breach of ethics."

"I'm no longer the Rutherfords' attorney, but that doesn't make a lot of difference to me. I came here to say something and I'm saying it. Phil Rutherford is a drug user and you put Dillon Rutherford in danger every moment he's been living with his father."

"What? Do you have proof?"

Quinn had to swallow his pride. "No."

The judge's face relaxed and she picked up a pen on her desk. "So this is an assumption on your part, because you're ticked off at Mr. Rutherford for firing you?"

"This has nothing to do with that."

She pointed the pen at him. "I think it does, Mr. Ross. Your conduct is out of line and I have no choice but to file a complaint. I can't believe you'd risk your career, your reputation over this."

Quinn rubbed his jaw, not moved by the criticism. "It's a little strange to me that a judge would award custody to a father because of the mother's job."

Judge Norcutt rose to her feet, her body stiff with rage. "Get out, Mr. Ross."

Quinn ignored her outrage. "How long have you been on the bench, Judge? Fifteen? Twenty years? A long while, and time enough to cross paths with the mighty Philip Rutherford Sr."

"What are you saying?"

"I'm saying that complaint thing goes both ways. I'm going to check into your background, and if I find the tiniest connection to Philip Rutherford Sr., I'm coming after you like a pit bull. And if my license is pulled I know a lot of good lawyers, like Mona Tibbs, who will happily take up the cause." Pivoting, he strolled toward the door.

"Mr. Ross."

He stopped and turned back.

"I don't respond well to threats," the judge said.

"Neither do I."

"Well then, let's agree to disagree," she suggested in a stiff tone. "And if you find any evidence Phil Rutherford is doing drugs, bring it to me and I'll reverse my decision immediately."

Quinn inclined his head. The good judge was guilty as hell and covering her ass six ways from Sunday, but Quinn took the forced olive branch. Now he had to uncover the evidence as quickly as possible.

So Dillon could be home with his mother for Christmas.

Chapter Sixteen

A week before Christmas Quinn feared he was running out of time. Levi was the best detective in the state and he still couldn't turn up anything on Phil. If the man was doing drugs, he was very good at covering his tracks.

Every day Quinn waited for disciplinary action to be taken against him, but so far he hadn't heard from the Texas Bar Association. Philip hadn't changed his mind, Quinn was sure of that. Judicial action took time, and it gave him the time he needed to end the custody battle over Dillon once and for all.

Lenny Skokel had been hired by the Rutherfords. A courier had picked up the files, but Quinn saved copies. Lenny was a trial lawyer without ethics, morals or character, who, for a big fee, would slice and dice Britt's life to shreds. After Lenny was finished, a judge wouldn't grant her custody of a puppy. Quinn couldn't let that happen. Time was now his enemy.

Grabbing his cell, he punched in Levi's number to find out if he was making any progress. Without warning, his door opened and Britt's ex walked in.

Quinn slowly placed his phone on the desk. "I don't believe you have an appointment, Phil," he said in his best don't-mess-with-me tone.

The man thumbed toward the front door. "The sign says you're closed until January 3."

"Yes, and that means I'm not seeing anyone."

Phil reared back on his heels, a smug expression on his face. "Instead of the third you should put forever. Dad's not going to let you practice law much longer."

"Philip is powerful but he doesn't run the Texas Bar."

"Don't be too sure about that."

Quinn clenched his jaw. "Is there a purpose for this visit?"

"Yeah. My new attorney says I have to inform Roslyn that I'm taking Dillon away for the holidays, and I thought you'd be the best person to deliver that information." A thread of accusation ran through each word.

Quinn ignored the finger-pointing tactics. "Has the judge signed off on this?"

"Of course. I wouldn't do anything illegal."

Yeah, right. How did Phil get that by Judge Norcutt? Quinn didn't have to think long about the answer. Philip Sr. Damn!

"Why don't *you* tell Ms. Davis?"

"Her lawyer filed a restraining order against me, and as I said, I'm not doing anything illegal."

Thank God Mona was a step ahead of the bastard. Quinn was seething at this turn of events and he had to get all the information he could. "What about Ms. Davis's visitation days?"

"She can have a few days with the boy when I return."

"When is that?"

"Whenever I please." A sly grin spread across Phil's face.

Quinn stood, his body coiled in anger, and he had to restrain himself from physically attacking Phil. "How many people did your dad pay off for that?"

"Go to hell." Phil's face suddenly darkened.

Quinn tried to reach a softer side of the man, if he had one. "Think about your son for a change. He'll miss his mother. You can't be that coldhearted."

"See that Roslyn gets the message." Phil paused for a second. "And tell her if she wants to spend Christmas with her son, she knows how to make that happen."

"You can't be serious."

The sly grin was back in place before Phil turned and walked to the door.

"Phil."

He glanced back.

"Does your father know your plans concerning Ms. Davis?"

"He doesn't need to know everything."

Sorry bastard. "This isn't over."

"Oh, yeah, it's over, and you lose big time, old friend." Phil sauntered out with a chilling laugh.

Quinn plopped into his chair and ran his hands over his face. How was he going to tell Britt she wasn't going to see her son for Christmas? Or…

He slammed his fist onto the desk, the blunt sound echoing within him. How had he let this happen? He'd thought he had things under control, but now everything was spiraling into a vortex of pain. How did he stop it? It was going to take a miracle.

After Quinn calmed down, he called Mona to make sure she was aware of what was going on, and then he had to call Britt. He thought of going to her apartment, but there were too many good and happy memories there. And he wasn't sure he was welcome.

THE UNIVERSITY WAS CLOSED for the holidays, so Britt worked as much as she could at the restaurant and planned her time around her visits with Dillon. From the university to the restaurant to the stores and streets, everything was decorated and lit up with the spirit of Christmas. People with shopping bags hurried everywhere. Christmas was almost here. Dillon's eyes grew big at the decorations and lights, but he wasn't crazy about Santa Claus. It was exciting showing him everything and watching his reaction.

She had come to grips with the fact that she would have to wait until the day after Christmas to celebrate the holiday with her son. It was just a day, and she would enjoy it no matter when it was. She wrapped one more present and placed it under the tree. Dillon was going to love the soft stuffed bear she'd found.

She was putting the wrapping paper away when her phone rang. She saw the caller ID and quickly picked up, her heart racing.

"Could you please come to my office?" Quinn asked, and his voice filled her with so much love, so much regret. It hit her how lonely she'd been without him.

"Yes," she replied, without even thinking about it. They had to talk. He gave her the address and she quickly changed into black slacks, a white turtleneck and heels. Her hand trembled as she applied lipstick. Oh, God, she had missed him so much, and she couldn't contain her excitement.

But she tried, for her own sanity.

FORTY MINUTES LATER SHE found his office. She'd never been here before. It was on the fifth floor of a professional building on Congress Avenue that catered primarily to lawyers. The decor was very contemporary: glass, stainless steel and strategically placed potted plants. There was a notice on Quinn's office that said it was closed, but she pushed open the heavy oak door and went in. Inside, warm wood greeted her, from the floor to the desks, and the walls were a muted gold with eye-catching Texas landscapes taking pride of place. It was a soothing and relaxing atmosphere.

She heard Quinn talking on the phone, and followed his voice. The door was ajar so she walked in. He was sitting at his desk, his white shirtsleeves rolled up to his elbows. The shirt was opened at the neck and she glimpsed swirls of blond hairs—hair she'd run her fingers through…. Her stomach tightened with need and her eyes went to his face. His hair was longer, curling into his collar, as if he hadn't had time to get it cut. The angular lines of his face were tight with worry.

Still talking, he waved her to a chair. She had no idea what he was saying. She was too busy soaking up his presence. Easing into a leather chair, she slipped off her wool coat and placed her purse on the floor. She waited with her breath wedged in her throat like a cotton ball.

"Sorry," Quinn said as he laid his cell down, his eyes on her. At his warm gaze, a ripple of awareness flowed through her. "How are you?"

She swallowed a portion of the cotton. "Fine. Wha-what's this about?"

"I had a visit from Phil."

"And?" She braced herself.

He leaned back. "First, I have to tell you I'm no longer Phil's attorney."

Her pulse leaped. She hadn't expected this. "What happened?"

He seemed to be measuring his words like he always did. "They wanted me to file for permanent custody of Dillon and I refused."

Her heart sank to the pit of her stomach. "Can they do that?" she asked tentatively. "They don't have any grounds to do something like that." Her eyes flew to his. "Do they?"

He pushed a folder on the desk toward her.

She jumped up and flipped through it, her temper rising at the contents. "What is this?"

"Fabricated evidence that you have a temper and sleep around."

She stumbled back into the chair, feeling a paralyzing fear grip her. But she fought it. She wasn't going to break over this. She'd fight with her last breath.

"Phil brought you this so-called evidence?"

"No. I've had it from the start."

That took what little air she had left in her lungs.

"I had a feeling Phil and his dad would try something like this. That's why I asked for you to trust me."

And she hadn't. Her pride took a big hit and words eluded her.

"I was chosen for this case because they knew you and I were rescued together from the flooding. They also have photos of us kissing at your door. Phil wants revenge and he's stopping at nothing."

It took a moment for her to process everything Quinn was saying. "They used your connection to the Rutherfords to get to me."

"Exactly."

"And…and our relationship has…"

"Given them more grounds to take your child and have me disbarred."

She tried to speak and couldn't. Finally, she managed to murmur, "I'm sorry."

"Doesn't matter." He brushed it off with a wave of his hand. "We have to think about Dillon now."

"What have they planned?"

"They hired Lenny Skokel, a high-powered trial lawyer, to file for permanent custody of Dillon."

"No, no, no!" She didn't even realize she was screaming until she heard her voice echoing through the room.

He came around the desk and squatted in front of her. "You remember how strong you were in the creek?"

She nodded.

"You need to find that strength now."

"C-can they take him?" Her voice cracked.

He reached for her hand and entwined his fingers with hers. "I'm asking you again to trust me. Can you do that?"

She nodded, knowing she trusted him more than anyone on earth.

"Good." He squeezed her hand. "There's more."

"What?"

"Phil is taking Dillon away for the holidays."

"He can't do that. It's not in the ruling."

"The judge signed off on it."

"What?" Britt was being hit so many times she felt as if she was in the creek again, fighting for her life. And her hero was right in front of her. Why hadn't she trusted him all along? Fear. Plain old fear. Just like she was feeling now.

She gathered herself quickly, and only one thing made sense. "If he takes Dillon, I'll never see him again." She held out her left hand. "Please have Levi remove this."

Quinn seemed taken aback. "What for?"

"I don't have many options. I'll have to take Dillon and run."

His eyes widened. "What about trusting me?"

She closed her own eyes as a pain shot through her. "I can't lose my baby."

He reached out, undid the clasp and removed the bracelet.

"How did you do that?" she gasped. "I thought it needed to be cut or something."

He shook his head. "No. It's just a bracelet."

"What?"

"A trick I played on the judge and the Rutherfords so you could have time alone with Dillon."

"But—but Levi had a map and…"

"GPS gadget to make it look real. You were free to run at any time, but you didn't. Now you can." He pushed himself to his feet. "Once you do that, you'll seal your fate. If they catch you, you'll never see your son again and you'll go to jail. That would devastate Carin and Ona. But it's your choice."

Her emotions were waffling and precariously close to snapping. But through the turmoil in her mind she heard the hurt in his voice, and that got to her. He'd risked his life to save hers in the creek, and now she had to repay the favor. She had to risk her very life to believe in him. To trust him.

"This isn't easy," she whispered. "I'm so afraid…."

"I know you are. I am, too." He leaned back against the desk and folded his arms across his chest. "Phil wanted me to tell you something else that might make this easier for you."

"What?" The cotton swelled in her throat.

"He said to tell Roslyn if she wants to spend Christmas with her son, she knows how to make that happen. Going back to Phil would solve your problem."

Her eyes shot to his. "Are you serious?"

He shrugged.

She stood on shaky legs, her strength returning full force. "I would never ever go back to that bastard."

"Then is it so hard to trust me?"

Without having to think about it she whispered, "No." They'd been on opposite sides for so long, but fear couldn't block what she felt for him. Fear couldn't block that she needed him. Fear couldn't block that once again he'd risked everything for her. "You might have a problem keeping me sane, though." She tilted her head. "You see, I have some of Ona's genes."

To keep from touching her, Quinn walked back around the desk. It would be so easy to take her into his arms and forget the giant elephant in the room—the Rutherfords. Quinn's and Britt's future, if they had one, had to wait. He had to focus all his attention on Phil.

He pulled a legal pad out of a drawer. "The only way to stop all this is to prove Phil is a user."

"What can I do?"

That's what he wanted—her full cooperation.

He sat down. "In the six months you were married to him, did you see any signs?"

"No." She resumed her seat. "That's why it was such a shock. But he did have a lot of mood swings that sometimes frightened me."

Quinn twisted the pen between his fingers. "Could he have just been experimenting that day because he was upset with you?"

"I don't think so. The woman said something like 'Get rid of your wife or I'm not coming back again.' It sounded as if she'd been in my bed before."

"Did you get a name?"

"Phil kept saying 'Shut up, Candy.'"

"Had you seen her before?"

Britt shook her head.

"Think, Britt. I need something. Did you notice anything about the room that was different?"

"I was only there a minute." She closed her eyes. "The bed was in disarray and on the nightstand were a couple of plastic packets of brownish stuff. A syringe was there, too. And a little square of purple that looked like matches from a bar."

"Was there any wording on it?"

"Black lines weaved through the purple and there was *e s* something. I didn't stick around to read the rest."

Quinn scribbled that on the pad. "Do you know of any bars Phil liked to frequent?"

"I thought he liked the country club where he plays golf. But I really never knew him."

Quinn watched the expression on her face and it twisted his gut. He wanted to give her some reassurance, but again he had no guarantees.

"This should help some." He tapped the pen on the pad. "Levi's good at taking one clue and uncovering evidence."

"How much time do we have?"

Quinn lifted his shoulders. "I have someone watching the condo. If he leaves with Dillon, I'll know." He stared at the pen. "But I don't look for him to make a move until next Friday. He's waiting to see how badly you want to keep your son." Quinn looked at her when he said the last.

She visibly trembled, her eyes holding his. "I trust you. I wish I had from the start."

His heart wobbled. "Thank you. This has been a difficult situation. I wanted to tell you about the file, but I was still hanging on to my ethics. Now it doesn't even matter. Philip Sr. has threatened to have me disbarred."

"Can he do that?"

"Oh, yeah. I left ethics behind the moment I looked into your dark eyes."

She bit her lip. "I…"

"You don't have to say anything. Let's concentrate on Dillon."

She picked up the bracelet, which he'd placed on the desk. "I believe this belongs to me."

He lifted an eyebrow at that. Why did she want it? He hoped it was for the reason he thought.

She reached for her coat. "Now I'm going to go visit Mona and—"

"I've already apprised her of the situation."

"Oh, good, then I'll just touch base with her." She picked up her purse and walked from the room with smooth elegant strides, her courage firmly in place. At the door, she said, "I'll wait to hear from you."

As she left, Quinn ran his hands over his face. He couldn't let her down. That miracle was within his reach. He just had to find it. And that might prove the biggest challenge of his law career.

Chapter Seventeen

Quinn knew he had a few days, and each hour counted. His sister called about Christmas, and with everything going on it had completely slipped his mind. He had to give Peyton some details to make her understand. She was outraged at the Rutherfords, but he assured her he was doing his best to rectify the situation. Why he might miss the family Christmas took a lot more explaining.

Finally, he told her he would try to make it. That was the best he could do. When he got off the phone, he went online and ordered gifts for the family, paying the extra postage to have them delivered to Peyton's house fully wrapped by Christmas Eve.

Levi was working on the lead Britt had given them. They finally concluded *e s* stood for an escort service, one that Phil probably frequented often. Levi was working overtime trying to locate the service Phil used.

Quinn spent his time staking out Phil's condo. Levi's sidekick, Butch, relieved him so he could catch a few hours sleep, shower and change. Quinn wanted someone watching the place at all times. The moment Phil left with Dillon, he had to know. He wasn't sure about the plan if that happened, but Phil wasn't getting on a plane with Dillon. That Quinn knew for sure.

Levi finally located the escort service with a girl named

Candy. He was having a meeting with her now—as a client. If Quinn was in a laughing mood, he'd find that funny. But Levi would take it as far as he had to to get the information they needed.

It was early in the morning on Christmas Eve and the neighborhood was quiet. All the houses and condos were decorated for the big day, but a lot of people had gone out of town for the holiday. Mostly retired people lived in the exclusive condos, so no children were out in the street playing.

To remain inconspicuous, Quinn had rented a vacant condo across the street. He had to sign a six-month lease to get the place, but the money was a minor issue and it had a perfect view of Phil's. Quinn rented a car so Phil wouldn't recognize his Mercedes parked in the garage. From the master bedroom he could see Phil's driveway. No one seemed to notice him or Butch coming or going. He sat in a straight-backed chair and watched.

A white Corvette drove into Phil's driveway. Jenna Lawson slid out and ran inside, carrying a small suitcase. She didn't knock or use a key, so obviously the door was open. Something was about to happen. Quinn didn't take his eyes off the place. In his peripheral vision he saw a large city bus stop at the end of the street. He hadn't realized the buses ran in this area. Stretching his shoulders, he eased the tired muscles and kept waiting. And waiting for Levi to call.

Sometimes it was hard staying awake, but Quinn forced himself to. The thermos of black coffee helped. He was taking a swig when something caught his eye. He blinked, not believing what he was seeing. Bonnie and Clyde were walking down the sidewalk, straight to Phil's door. Damn it! What were they up to?

He reached for his cell and punched in Britt's number.

"Get over to Phil's right away. Ona's here," he said, before she could get in a word.

"Damn it!" he cursed, leaping out of the chair and running down the stairs. Ona and Enzo had just blown everything to hell. He didn't know how he was going to explain his presence, but he had no choice but to get them out of there.

He went out the back way, crossed the street farther down and ran like hell toward Phil's. When he was about twenty feet away, Phil opened the door.

"What the hell do you want?"

"I brought my great-grandson a gift for Christmas," Ona replied.

"And you think I'm going to let you give it to him?"

"Why not? You got somethin' to hide?"

"Go away," Phil shouted, and moved to close the door. But Ona was ready for him. She pushed past him, using her big purse as a shield. Enzo was on her heels.

"Get out of my house," Phil shouted. "Or I'm calling the cops."

Quinn rushed in and all eyes turned to him.

"Lookie, Enzo, Mr. Hotshot has arrived."

"Get them out of here," Phil growled. Quinn noticed he had on a robe and pajamas.

"I'm not going anywhere until I see my great-grandson," Ona threatened, clutching a bag in one hand and her purse in the other.

"You know," Enzo said to Phil, "I have connections to the mob, and with one phone call I can have you taken out like yesterday's rotten garbage."

"You're a senile old man with one foot in the grave," Phil told him.

Enzo swung his cane and hit him on his kneecap, wood

hitting bone with a sharp crack. Phil grabbed his leg, screaming, "You son of a bitch. You son of a bitch!"

Quinn felt as if he was in a comedy skit, especially when Jenna came running in wearing a short, silky, black negligee. "What's going on in here?" She glanced around. "Phil, who are these people?"

"Call the cops," Phil moaned, holding his leg.

"I don't think you want to do that," Quinn said, trying to calm things down.

Undeterred by Phil's threat, Ona gave Jenna the once-over and said, "Lookie, Enzo, here's a stripper for you."

"I'm not a stripper," Jenna declared hotly, trying to cover her breasts, which were spilling out of her gown.

"Sure look like one, honey."

"Nah, Ona, she's too skinny," Enzo piped.

"I'm not skinny!" Jenna turned on him.

Phil straightened, his face dark. "Quinn, you better get them out of here now."

Before Quinn could move or speak, Britt appeared in the doorway, out of breath. Phil's eyes swung to her and his face cleared. This was what he was waiting for, Quinn thought.

As well as jeans and dress boots, she wore a red knit top covered with a brown corduroy jacket. Her hair was down, framing her beautiful face. Her dark eyes flashed with irritation. She took in the situation with one glance. "Let's go, Onnie, Enzo."

"Sorry, my pretty, I'm not going anywhere until I see Dillon. I have his Christmas gift." Ona held up the bag.

Quinn could see Britt was calculating her next move. He could almost read her mind. She had nothing to lose. "Well, then. Let's give it to him."

"I don't think so," Phil said in a threatening voice.

Jenna moved closer to him, linking her arm through his. "For heaven sakes, Phil, it's Christmas."

That put Phil in a difficult situation—look bad in front of his girlfriend or let Britt and Ona see Dillon? But Britt didn't give him time to make up his mind. She took her grandmother's arm and headed for the stairs.

And Phil did nothing.

Silence enveloped the four people standing in the entry. Finally, Enzo looked at Phil. "You got any beer?"

"Go to hell," Phil snapped, and walked into the living area.

"Guess that means no," Enzo remarked.

Quinn frowned at the old man, and then wanted to laugh. But it wasn't a day for laughing.

BRITT HUGGED, KISSED AND touched her little boy. His bubbles of delight melted her heart. "Mommy loves you, Dilly bear." Britt was grateful for this moment on Christmas Eve with her son.

Onnie pulled a big bag from her purse. "Enough of that. Let's put Dillon in here and get the hell out."

"What?" Britt stopped bouncing her baby.

"That's what Enzo and me planned. We'd put the baby in here—it's not plastic if that's what you're worried about. We'll go out the back way. That bastard will never know and Dillon will be with us for Christmas."

Britt gave Dillon a long kiss and placed him in his bed. "We're not putting Dillon in anything. We're not stealing him. That makes us criminals. I'm getting him back the legal way." Quinn was right. She had to trust him. Running away with Dillon was not an option. She could clearly see that. "Give Dillon your gift."

"I didn't bring a gift." Onnie scrunched up her face. "Aren't you listening? We plan to take him."

Britt groaned. "What were you going to do about the nanny?"

"That skinny thing? She wouldn't be a problem."

"Let's go, Onnie." Britt turned her grandmother toward the door. "This little stunt is over."

"You're getting more and more like your mother," Onnie grumbled.

"Thank you." She stopped at the door and blew Dillon a kiss. He whined and she steeled herself to go. "Mommy will see you soon," she called, closing the door and trying very hard not to cry.

Debi was in the hall and went back in.

Britt forced herself to walk away, though all she could think was this might be the last time she'd see her son.

Her stomach cramped, but she was trusting Quinn with everything in her.

When they reached the bottom of the stairs, Quinn and Enzo were still in the foyer. Phil and his girlfriend were sitting in the living room. When Phil saw her, he got up and came forward. Britt had to force herself to face him.

"I hope you enjoyed your visit, Roslyn, because it will be your last for a while."

Something in the tone of his voice, or maybe something about her kick-butt grandmother's attitude, had her stepping closer to him. She'd had it. She wasn't going to cry or beg. She was going to fight.

"I thought I really loved you once, but you shattered every illusion I had about love. What type of man would take a child from his mother? Only the very worst kind, and you've proved it over and over again."

His face blanched and she knew she'd hit a nerve. She could feel Quinn's presence to her right and it gave her the courage to say what she had to. "How you can listen to your own son cry so heartbreakingly for his mother, and do nothing, is beyond me. I guess it shows where your priorities are. They've never been with Dillon or me. You're only concerned about yourself."

She drew a quick breath. "And to use your own son as bait to lure me back is beyond contempt."

"What?" Phil's girlfriend cried, but Britt ignored her.

"I will never come back to you, so do your evil best with threats of keeping Dillon from me. Bribe all the judges you need to, but wherever you go I will find you. I'll call newspapers, TV stations, radio stations, and give interviews exposing you as the bastard you are. You will never keep my son. That's a promise." She turned and walked from the condo with her dignity intact.

Outside, she clung to her grandmother. "You told him, my pretty." Onnie stroked her hair.

Britt caught Quinn's concerned gaze and she went to him. "Do you have anything?"

"Not yet," he told her, still blown away by her courage. Phil had looked like a battered fighter brought down by a surprise opponent. "Levi has located the hooker Phil was with the day you found him. I'm hoping to hear something shortly."

"Call me when you do." She leaned in close. "Now I have to take Bonnie and Clyde home and once again try to explain this to my mother."

He wanted to wrap his arms around her and never let her go. Instead, he reached for her hand, twisting the bracelet she'd put back on. When he felt her cold fingers, he realized just how afraid she was. "You were awesome. Don't lose that strength."

"It's Christmas Eve," she murmured in a small voice, and leaned against him. His heart lurched at her sadness.

I love you. But he couldn't say the words. Not now. The cool December breeze blew against them and he kissed the top of her head. She sighed and then went to help Ona and Enzo into her car.

He lifted a hand in goodbye and strolled down the walk with a heart as heavy as a bowling ball. Getting to his rented condo proved to be tricky. Several people passing by gave him odd glances, so he hurried around the back, slipping in without Phil noticing or anyone calling the cops. Not that Rutherford was looking. Quinn suspected the man had his hands full trying to explain Britt's remark about luring her back. Jenna had not been pleased.

The condo was empty, but Quinn kept food in the refrigerator. He grabbed a soft drink and a bag of nuts and went back to his post. Again everything was quiet.

Quinn pulled out his phone and sent a text message to Levi. It was one word: *hurry*. He didn't understand what was taking so damn long. He stretched and walked around the room, keeping his eyes on Phil's.

The day dragged. The sky grew cloudy and the wind rattled through the large oak outside the window. Quinn could hear a limb brushing against the roof. The swishing sound helped count away the time.

Sitting down again, he thought this was a hell of a way to spend Christmas Eve. And his sister was probably so pissed she was never going to speak to him again. His mother...well, he'd just as soon not think about that.

His cell buzzed and he yanked it out of his pocket. He cursed when he saw the name. Deidre.

He clicked on, knowing she'd keep trying if he didn't. "Hello."

"Hi, Quinn. Are you busy?"

"Yes."

"I'm at my dad's and I'm bored out of my mind. Let's go to a nightclub or something."

She didn't even hear what he'd said. He took a long,

hard breath. "Deidre, please don't call me again. It's over, and you might think about spending some time with your father. It's Christmas Eve."

There was a long pause. "Are you kidding?"

"No."

Another long pause, as if she was trying to figure out why he'd made such a suggestion. "Have you found someone else?"

"Yes. Have a Merry Christmas." He clicked off and slipped the phone into his shirt pocket. He'd found the most wonderful woman, one he'd give his life for. That's why he was sitting in an empty condo staring out a window when he should be celebrating with his family.

Suddenly his whole world was Britt and Dillon.

They were his family.

For the first time he wondered if Britt felt the same way.

BY MIDAFTERNOON QUINN grew weary of waiting for something to happen. There was no activity at Phil's. If they were leaving for the holiday, there were no signs.

Where in the hell was Levi? He sent another text, wanting to throw the phone out the window. Instead, he stood and stretched again, hating the waiting. Suddenly the front door was flung open and Jenna ran to her car, buttoning her blouse, tears streaming down her face. The Corvette revved up and spun out of the driveway, tires squealing.

What was that about? Obviously, they'd had a big argument. Quinn resumed his seat, his eyes glued to Phil's. About thirty minutes later, the garage door went up and he put luggage into the backseat of the car. The nanny came out and placed baby things inside, and then the door went down.

Phil was getting ready to leave, so why didn't he leave

the door up? That puzzled Quinn. He was ready to sprint downstairs as soon as Phil got into his car with Dillon. But it didn't happen. Quinn kept waiting.

He was so engrossed with the scene that he didn't hear Levi come in. He jumped straight up when the P.I. spoke.

"Where in the hell have you been? I've sent a dozen messages." Quinn's voice was sharp with frustration.

Levi pulled up the extra chair. "Calm down. This wasn't easy."

Quinn blew out a breath and plopped back into his seat. "What happened?"

"I didn't want to spook 'em so I had to appear as a normal customer."

"You didn't…?" Quinn lifted an eyebrow.

"Hell, no. I'm not sleeping with a hooker, not even for you." Levi stretched out his legs. "Seems Candy is very busy, and I had to wait. And the whole time the madam was shoving all these other women at me. I couldn't call or text because they were watching me like a hawk. The business is exclusive, very private, very confidential. I only got in by using Phil's name."

"And?"

"When I finally got to see her, I told her I wanted what Phil got because he always bragged about her. She was leery at first and had to go talk to the madam. What it comes down to is sex and drugs. Phil's preference is heroin at a whopping cost of five grand. I told her no way and got the hell out of there."

Suddenly, Quinn's chest felt lighter. "You have this on tape, right?"

"Damn straight. I had to hide the mic in my hat but I got every word she said."

Quinn reached for his jacket on the back of his chair.

"I'm going to call Judge Norcutt. You keep an eye on the place. Phil put luggage in his car a little while…" His voice trailed off as he saw the nanny come out, get in her car and drive away.

"What the hell?" Quinn ran a hand through his hair. "Why is she leaving?"

"There are two nannies," Levi replied. "Maybe the other one is on the way."

Quinn shook his head. "Something's not right. I don't like Dillon being in the house without the nanny."

"Relax," Levi advised. "Let's see what happens."

Quinn eased back into his chair, knowing Phil wouldn't physically harm his own son. In the meantime Quinn tried the judge's number and was told she wasn't taking calls until after the holidays. Damn it! He'd have to find a way around that.

Darkness crawled in like a lazy cat settling over the neighborhood. A light was on downstairs and one upstairs. Otherwise there was no activity at Phil's. No other nanny arrived and Phil didn't get in his car and leave.

Quinn stood. "I'm going over there. Something's wrong." He could feel it in his gut.

"I'm right behind you," Levi said. "But first I'm calling the police so we do everything legally."

When they reached the front door, a police car drove up. Quinn rang the bell. No response. He called on his cell. No one answered.

"A baby's inside and no one's responding," Quinn told the officers.

"Let me call my supervisor." One officer stepped away to talk on his phone. The other one searched around outside, looking for a way in.

"We have permission to kick in the door." The officer put away his phone. And the two uniformed men gave it their best shot, but the door was strong and heavy. Quinn and Levi gave them a hand and it took the strength of all four men to bring the door down.

Quinn was the first inside. He stopped short in the living room. Phil lay on the sofa, a needle stuck in his arm.

"Oh, my God!" Quinn didn't know if he was dead or alive.

Chapter Eighteen

"Dillon!"

Quinn shot up the stairs as an officer called for an ambulance. When he reached the landing, he heard loud wails, and bolted through the nursery door. Dillon stood up in his crib, holding on to the railing, crying his little heart out.

"Hey, buddy." Quinn lifted him out and Dillon quieted down, rubbing his wet eyes. Quinn realized that wasn't the only thing wet. Dillon needed a diaper change. Grabbing a clean one from a bag on the end of the crib, he laid Dillon in the bed and removed the soiled diaper and his all-in-one pajamas.

"Ma-ma-ma-ma," Dillon cooed as Quinn scooted the fresh diaper beneath him.

"Bear with me, buddy. I'm new at this." Oh, the diaper had tabs. How efficient. All the time he dressed Dillon he tried not to think about the situation downstairs. How could Phil do that? And why would he?

"Ma-ma-ma-ma." Dillon waved his arms around.

"I'm taking you to her just as soon as I can." He gathered Dillon, freshly dressed, into his arms just as a middle-aged woman with a large bag entered.

"I'm Gina Hardy with Child Protective Service. I'm here to take the boy."

"No," Quinn said, wondering where in the hell she'd

come from so quickly. But then he remembered CPS was always notified when a child was involved. "He has a mother who's waiting for him."

"Sorry." She shook her head. "Phil Rutherford has custody, and until I get a court order saying otherwise the baby goes with me."

"Listen, this child needs to be with his mother. It's Christmas."

"You think I want to be working on Christmas?" She lifted an eyebrow. "If I don't follow the rules, I could lose my job."

Quinn knew about the rules. He was a lawyer. Reluctantly, he handed over Dillon. "Where can I reach you? I'll be picking him up as soon as possible."

While juggling Dillon, she pulled out a card from her coat pocket. "It's Christmas Eve. You're not going to get a judge tonight or tomorrow."

"Don't bet on it, Ms. Hardy." He kissed Dillon's head. "Hang tight, little one, you're going home for Christmas."

Placing Dillon in his bed, she said, "Consider yourself a miracle worker, huh?"

"No. Just a damn good lawyer."

"Heaven help us." She started to collect Dillon's things.

Quinn let that slide and looked at the card. "You can be reached at this number at all times?"

"Yes," she replied, taking the card and turning it over. "That's my address. He'll have to stay with me until after Christmas. Then I'll find a foster home for him."

"Don't bother." Quinn swung toward the door. "I'll see you later."

"Yeah, right…" Her words followed him out the door.

Downstairs, Phil was being wheeled out of the condo on a stretcher. "Is he alive?" Quinn asked Levi.

"The paramedic found a pulse and they're getting him to an E.R."

Quinn ran both hands through his hair. "Why did he do something like that with Dillon right upstairs?"

"You can never tell with a drug user," Levi said. "They're unpredictable."

"Mr. Ross."

Quinn turned to an officer, who had a lot of questions. Quinn told him everything he knew about Jenna and the nanny leaving, and what Levi had uncovered about Candy. The officer wrote everything down and they moved out of the way for the crime unit to gather evidence.

"If that's it for the night—" Levi straightened his hat "—I'm going home. Someone told me it was Christmas."

"Yep. It's slipping right by us," Quinn remarked.

"Call if you need anything."

"I'm going to break down a judge's door on Christmas Eve. Want to come with me?"

"I'll pass," Levi replied as they walked outside into the cool night air. "But call if you need me to get you out of jail."

Quinn forced a smile. "Thanks for all your help."

"Anytime." Levi strolled across the street to his truck, parked in the garage of the condo.

Quinn drew a hard breath. The wind now rustled through the oaks with a distant, chilling sound that went right through him. What a hell of a way to spend Christmas. He wanted to call Britt, just to hear her voice, but he had to tell her this kind of news in person. And he couldn't tell her CPS had Dillon. That would be too painful. He wouldn't call until he had good news.

Pulling out his cell, he punched in Philip's number. He

had no idea if the man was in Austin or Colorado, but he had to know about his son.

"What do you want, Quinn?" The gruff voice came in clearly. "You're not getting any favors from me."

Quinn ignored the tone. "It's about Phil."

"What about him? Is he with you? He was supposed to have been here three hours ago."

"Where are you?"

"At my house in Rob Roy in Austin. My wife's kids are here for Christmas and we're waiting on Phil. He won't answer his damn phone. You better not have pulled anything."

So Phil wasn't going out of town, just to his father's. It was all a ruse to get Britt to capitulate.

"Phil's had an accident." Quinn didn't know how else to say it. "He's in the E.R. at Saint David's. You need to get there as soon as you can."

"What kind of accident?"

"Just get there." Quinn clicked off, not willing to say anything else. Philip wouldn't believe him, anyway. He had to find out for himself.

Quinn ran across the street and grabbed his briefcase out of his car. Standing at the large island in the kitchen at the condo, he withdrew papers and went over them, writing in dates. He'd had the papers drawn up for days and now he was going to use them.

When he'd finished, he called the judge again, but got the same annoying message. He then called Denise. She knew everything about the lawyers and judges in Austin. Within minutes he had the good judge's home address.

He closed his briefcase, locked the condo and headed for his car. Backing out, he took a last look at Phil's house. A sadness pulsed inside him and he wondered whether, if he had gone over sooner, he would have been able to stop him. Probably not. Quinn had a feeling Phil was lost the day he'd started using heroin. Still, it wasn't an easy thing to deal with. Quinn hoped he'd make it.

As he drove, Quinn couldn't stop thinking about Phil, and he found himself heading to the hospital. An antiseptic smell greeted him as he walked though the sliding doors. Nurses and doctors hurried here and there, and Quinn moved out of their way.

He spotted Philip and several family members he didn't recognize waiting in a secluded area. When Philip spotted him, he hurried over.

"How's Phil?"

"He died a little while ago," Philip said without emotion, without one ounce of sadness.

"I'm sorry." Quinn felt a tightness in his chest.

"You tried to tell me and I wouldn't listen."

"You had no idea?"

"He had some problems in college, but I thought that was all behind him." The man's voice cracked, the first sign he was holding everything inside like the strong man he was supposed to be. "The girlfriend, whatever her name is, said they started doing drugs in the early afternoon, but Phil wouldn't stop. He said he wanted to take the edge off. He was meeting my new wife and her two kids for the first time. The son works in the U.S. Attorney General's office and the daughter is a special prosecutor for the FBI. Both Harvard graduates. Both outstanding young people. I told Phil he'd better get his act together. I guess I pushed too hard." Philip blinked as if he had something in his eye. "The girlfriend said she tried to get him to stop, and he hit her. She left. The nanny said they packed everything in the car, ready to leave, and then Phil changed his mind. When she asked questions, he ordered her out. I guess he was bent on a night of destruction."

"With his son upstairs."

"Yeah." Philip wiped a hand across his face. "I'm sorry about that."

The man didn't ask about Dillon or where he was. That irked Quinn. "A CPS worker took Dillon. I'm on my way to Judge Norcutt to get a court order to return the boy to his mother."

Philip only nodded.

"Please don't throw up any roadblocks, because you don't want to meet me in court on this one. I might get a reprimand or have my license revoked by the Texas Bar, but—"

Philip held up a hand. "I'm not doing anything about you or the boy. I don't have any strength left." He glanced back at the waiting group. "Now I have to try and explain this horrendous night to my new family."

That seemed to be the man's top priority, but Quinn wanted to be clear. "Dillon stays with his mother...permanently."

"Yes...yes."

Quinn watched a man he'd once idolized, and thought how money and power could destroy character, morals and families. Philip had aged ten years in the last few minutes. His face was haggard, his vision dull, and he would spend the rest of his life wondering what he could have done differently to save his son.

"I am sorry about Phil," was all Quinn could say.

"Thank you. I know you mean that."

"Yes, sir." Quinn walked away, hoping that Philip's new family could help him find a measure of peace.

TWENTY MINUTES LATER HE knocked on the judge's door. A young woman in her thirties opened it.

"Quentin Ross to see Judge Norcutt," he said without preamble.

"I'm sorry. She's not seeing anyone but family tonight."

Quinn stepped into the foyer without an invitation. Voices and laughter could be heard in another room. "Tell her or I'm interrupting the party."

The woman scowled at him, but turned and went into a room on the left. In a minute the judge came out, dressed in a white gown and heels. She looked different than the stern official he was used to.

"What is this, Mr. Ross? I resent you interrupting my evening."

"Phil Rutherford died of a heroin overdose tonight." He didn't feel the need to sugarcoat it.

"What?" She sank into a high-back chair next to a small entry table.

He laid the custody papers on the table next to her. "CPS took Dillon Rutherford. All I need from you is your signature on this order returning full custody of Dillon to his mother."

"Of course. I'm so sorry."

He handed her a pen, not willing to be lenient. "You should be. You took a baby away from a loving mother and put him in the hands of a drug addict."

She scribbled her name in the appropriate places and stood. "I made the best call I could with the evidence I had. And you, Mr. Ross, were the Rutherfords' attorney."

He picked up the papers. "Not by choice. But yes, ma'am, there's enough blame to go around." He turned toward the door. "Have a nice Christmas."

In his car, he glanced at his watch. Eleven o'clock. He hoped Ms. Hardy was still up.

BRITT SAT ON THE SOFA in the dark with only the Christmas tree lights on, her cell clutched in her hand. Why hadn't Quinn called? What had happened? The questions went round and round in her brain like naughty children on a merry-go-round.

She stretched out and rested her head on a cushion. Dillon's toys were under the tree waiting for him. But would he ever open them? A sob wedged in her throat and she swallowed.

Quinn, please call.

No news was good news, she kept telling herself.

Flipping onto her side, she forced herself to think about something else. Her mother had wanted to spend the night, but Britt made her and Onnie go home. She planned to leave early in the morning to spend Christmas with them. Tonight she had to stay in Austin so she'd know if Phil had taken Dillon out of the state.

Quinn would call.

She just had to wait.

Strangely, her mother wasn't angry with Onnie for pulling another stunt. Mainly because it had given Britt a chance to see Dillon on Christmas Eve. Carin had said that if she had known what Onnie was going to do, she would have helped her. They laughed about that. Britt and Carin agreed that they were going to be more lenient with Onnie, and maybe, just maybe, she wouldn't feel the need to pull such stunts. Knowing Onnie, though, she would always keep their lives interesting.

Britt went into the bedroom and grabbed Quinn's pillow. She still hadn't washed the pillowcase. It reminded her of him. Taking it back to the sofa, she curled up with it. She breathed in his manly scent and drifted off to sleep.

The faint ringing of a doorbell woke her. She sat up, pushing her hair out of her eyes. *Was that…?* The doorbell rang again. *It was.* She shot to the entry and glanced through the peephole, and her heart hammered loudly in her ears. "Oh, my. Oh, my." She couldn't get the door opened fast enough.

Quinn, looking a little ragged and tired, but gorgeous, stood there holding the most beautiful sight in the world. Her baby—Dillon—was asleep on his shoulder.

"Oh, my baby." She scooped him out of Quinn's arms and they walked into the apartment. Britt sat on the sofa, smoothing Dillon's hair and loving the feel of him.

"What happened?" she asked.

Quinn took a long breath and told her a story that sent chills up her spine.

"He's…he's dead?" She could hardly say the words.

"Yes. You were right all along. He's been doing drugs for a long time. The judge awarded you full custody of Dillon, so you don't have to worry anymore."

Britt's eyes met Quinn's in the light from the tree. "Thank you for being there for Dillon. And for me."

Quinn glanced at the tree. "Dillon is where he should be, home with you and ready for Christmas."

"I'll never be able to thank you enough."

"Just be happy."

She kissed Dillon's cheek. "When you rescued me from the flooding creek, I thought of you as my hero." Her gaze caught his. "You're always going to be my hero. My Christmas hero."

He bent down and touched her lips with his. "Merry Christmas," he whispered.

Before she could respond, Dillon stirred and rubbed his eyes, whining.

"Time to put Dilly bear to bed." She stood, rubbing her son's back. "It's going to feel so good to see him back in his crib. Thank you." She smiled at Quinn and walked into the bedroom.

She changed Dillon's diaper and tucked him in, staring at her Christmas miracle. All because of Quinn. Now she just wanted him to hold her forever. She hurried back into the living room and stopped short. Quinn wasn't there. He wasn't in the kitchen. He was gone.

Her heart sank. Why had he left? He was tired, she knew. He'd been watching Phil's condo for days. Wrapping her arms around her waist, she sat on the sofa again. What a horrendous night, and Quinn had been there to see it all. That had to have been mentally and physically draining. And he had done it all for her.

Phil was dead. That took some getting used to. Although she had grown to despise him, she had also loved him once, and felt a deep sadness for the life he'd thrown away. She would remember the Phil who'd been fun, generous and full of dreams when she'd first met him. That would be the man she'd tell Dillon about.

The nightmare was over. But there was still an emptiness inside her. She had her son. She had her life back.

But she didn't have Quinn.

The Christmas lights blinked at her. Quinn had been working around the clock on her case. He probably hadn't had time to put up a tree.

Without thinking about it, and going with her heart, she went into the utility room for a plastic container and began to take down her tree.

QUINN WAS DOG TIRED WHEN he let himself into his house. He didn't bother turning on any lights as he made his way to his study. Sinking into his leather chair, he ran his hands over his face. What a night. What a horrible, horrible night.

The only light shining through was that Britt and Dillon were back together. Their Christmas would be complete.

He'd wanted to stay at her place tonight, but too much had happened for him to take that leap. They had to adjust to the sadness of the situation and learn to live with it. He'd call her after the holiday, if he lasted that long.

He wanted to offer her the world. She deserved no less after what she'd been through with Phil. Quinn knew he was at the crossroads of his life. His work wasn't exciting or exhilarating anymore. The violence and abuse had taken its toll.

Glancing around the study, he could feel his father's presence. That gentle, soothing nature of his was all around Quinn. As a young man he'd wanted his father to be forceful, dynamic, a take-charge type of person, but he wasn't, so Quinn had emulated men like Philip Rutherford who fit that bill. How wrong he had been! He'd traded gold for fool's gold. And that was never more apparent than tonight.

He picked up a stone from Egypt his dad used as a paperweight. Rubbing his thumb over it, he said, "I'm not cut out to be a cutthroat defense attorney. I'm good at it, but it puts a strain on my heart. You knew it would get to me, didn't you?"

He stood and flexed his stiff shoulders, knowing he had already made a decision about his future. A future that included happiness. And a family.

Heading for the stairs, he decided to shower and catch a few hours sleep before going to Peyton's for Christmas.

As he laid his weary body on the mattress ten minutes later, the doorbell rang. "What the…?"

He grabbed a robe and some warm slippers and made his way to the foyer. Glancing through the glass, he frowned but quickly opened the door. Britt stood there, holding a sleeping Dillon.

"What's wrong?" he asked, pulling them inside out of the cold.

"You left. That's what's wrong," she replied, her eyes sparkling like stars in a pitch-black sky. "And heroes don't leave."

"What?" He was thrown for a second.

"Heroes don't leave," she repeated.

"They don't?" He felt a grin spreading across his face like butter on a hot biscuit. He was still her hero. That said everything he wanted to hear.

"No," she said huskily. "They ride off into the sunset and live happily ever after."

He stroked her cheek with the back of his hand and loved the way her eyes darkened when he did that. Cupping her face, he kissed her with all the fire and love inside him. "I love you, Britt Davis," he said against her trembling lips. "I just thought it was too soon, with everything that had happened."

"I love you, too," she whispered back, and the words had never sounded so heartfelt, so everlasting. "I can't get through this night without you." She rested her forehead against his chin, clutching Dillon in her arms. "Would you please get Dillon's Pack 'n Play out of the car so I can kiss you like there's no tomorrow?"

"Yes, ma'am. Hold that thought...."

It took him a few minutes to get the thing out of the trunk, and he hurried back to her. Setting it up by the gas fireplace, he said, "There's a tree and presents jammed into the backseat of your car."

She kissed Dillon and laid him in the bed, tucking a blanket around him. The baby never moved or made a sound. "Of course, we can't have Christmas without a tree and gifts for Dillon."

"Did you take down your tree?" He turned on the fire and it roared to life.

She straightened, her eyes twinkling. "Crazy, huh?"

He locked his hands behind her back and whirled her onto the sofa. "Crazy and wonderful. Just like you." He took her lips once again and she wrapped her arms around him, and he lost himself in her sweetness, her love and the heated emotions they'd shared. Her fingers slipped inside his robe to his chest, and his body tightened with uncontrollable need. He caressed her hand. "I was feeling so down, but now I'm on top of the world."

She kissed his knuckles. "Me, too. Hold me, please."

He gathered her against his chest and stroked her hair.

"I'm going to trust you forever, my hero," she whispered sleepily.

The flickering fire cast a glow over them, and he looked into her eyes and knew he'd found exactly what he'd been searching for—the woman to fill his heart, his life, with love.

"I'm going to love you every day like there's no tomorrow."

She laughed, and the old house seemed to sigh as a new era of Rosses began.

Epilogue

One year later…

Britt straightened an ornament on the eight-foot Douglas fir that stood in front of the French windows looking out into the backyard. Brightly wrapped packages rested beneath the tree. The house was fully decorated, with garlands on the staircase and mantel. Poinsettias added color and the lights sparkled invitingly. They were ready for Christmas.

This year was different.

They were happy, and together.

Last Christmas was a painful memory that time and love had managed to diminish. The past year had been a time of change. A year of healing, discovering new goals and dreams, and living life to the fullest.

She and Quinn had married a month after she'd come to his lovely home in the middle of the night to give him her heart. She never went back to her apartment to live. Their life together had started that moment.

They'd talked about their future, slept in each other's arms and awoke in time to put up the tree before Dillon stirred. They'd embraced change together. Quinn was back in school to get his doctorate so he could teach on the university level. She was in school, too. She was now a mother and a student, and she loved it. Quinn would eventually phase out his law practice and teach full time. But for now he was still helping people who needed him.

She glanced at her watch. He had a meeting with the dean, but he should have been home by now. Where was he? It was Christmas Eve.

Dillon, dressed in his new slacks and white shirt, knelt on the hardwood floor, playing with a train set Quinn had bought him. Quinn had taken him to get his hair cut, and she'd combed it neatly, but knew it wouldn't stay that way long. Dillon was a typical little boy.

He watched the train go round and round, and then stopped it and started it again, over and over. Content. Happy. That's what she wanted for her son.

The first couple of months after Phil's death had been hard on Dillon. He'd cried if Britt was out of his sight. He was fussy and threw temper tantrums. Young as he was, he knew something was wrong in his world.

Quinn made the difference. The two bonded immediately, and Dillon didn't cry if she left him with Quinn. Gradually, Dillon became more and more secure, and today he was a completely different child. She would probably always blame herself that her baby had to go through such trauma. But she vowed from here on his life would be as idyllic as she could make it.

A car engine purred in the driveway. Dillon's head shot up. "Dad-dy," he shouted, and was off and running for the back door.

Britt followed more slowly. Quinn had adopted Dillon. They kept waiting for Philip to throw a wrench in the works, but they never heard a word from him. He'd sold the Rutherford firm to his partners, and he'd also sold Phil's condo and the house in Rob Roy, moving to Colorado with his new family. Quinn said that he didn't think the man would ever return to Austin.

Dillon would grow up with a father who loved him and who Dillon adored. Britt would tell him about his real father only if he asked. Now he was Dillon Ross to the world. She was grateful for that.

She stopped short in the kitchen. Quinn squatted with Dillon in one arm and a dog that looked like a Jack Russell terrier in the other.

"Mommy, doggie," Dillon said, pointing to the dog.

"I see."

"Let me explain." Quinn's eyes twinkled as she'd seen them do so many times, and her heart melted. He stood, and his gorgeous blue eyes roamed over her red dress and heels, igniting the flame that always flared between them. "Whoa, are we going somewhere?"

"Don't change the subject."

He wrapped an arm around her waist and tugged her to him. Her body welded to every strong masculine line of his. "This feels good," he murmured against her face.

"Mmm. So good." She moved against him and loved his instant response. "But first things first. Why did the dean want to see you?"

"A professor was taken unexpectedly ill, and that's why the dean was in his office on Christmas Eve. He asked me to monitor one of the professor's classes until he returns, sort of an intern thing. I start when the semester begins again, and balance the class with my studies."

She kissed him. "Wonderful."

He rested his forehead against hers. "I'm changing my whole life all because of you, and it feels right. You made me realize that change isn't so bad, especially when it makes me a better person, a better husband and father.

You made me want everything out of my reach—home, family and love. With you everything is possible."

"Oh, Quinn." She looked into his eyes. "I love you and I'm so glad I found the perfect hero."

He kissed the tip of her nose.

Dillon giggled, rolling around with the dog on the tiled floor, his shirttail untucked from his pants and his shoes untied. And she'd just dressed him.

"Now about the dog, Mr. Hero."

"Well, the dean had him in his office. He'd bought him for his grandson for Christmas, but the son reminded him that his wife has allergies, so they couldn't accept him. Luckily, the grandson didn't know. The dean was trying to find the dog a good home. We were talking about getting Dillon a puppy, so I offered to take him."

Dillon squealed with delight as the dog licked his face.

"See? They're already friends."

Britt stroked Quinn's face. "You're such a good father."

His eyes darkened. "You keep doing that and we won't get out of the kitchen."

"Mom and Onnie are on the way to spend the night, so they'll be here when Dillon opens his presents in the morning. And they're bringing food."

"Ah, food or passion?" He leaned his head back and pretended to consider it. She laughed.

Quinn loved her musical laugh, and he loved her. She filled all the empty places in his heart and in his life. She made the old house come alive again. She made him feel alive. And loneliness was nowhere in sight.

He kissed her again. "What's the plan with Peyton?"

"We're having a late dinner tomorrow at her house with

your mother. It's all arranged." Britt's sexy mouth curved playfully. "I'm a good wife."

"How did I get so lucky?"

"You jumped into a raging creek to save my life. Now you're stuck with me and my dysfunctional family."

He grinned. "I wouldn't have it any other way."

The doorbell rang.

"Nana, Onnie," Dillon cried, and ran for the front door with the dog on his heels.

Quinn cupped Britt's face and kissed her deeply. "Merry Christmas, Mrs. Ross, and may we never come unstuck."

She smiled, and Quinn took her hand and fingered the bracelet that she never took off. They'd weathered the storm. Even though life wouldn't always be smooth, they would continue to find shelter in each other's arms.

* * * * *

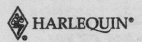

HARLEQUIN®

COMING NEXT MONTH

Available January 11, 2011

REQUEST YOUR FREE BOOKS!
2 FREE NOVELS PLUS 2 FREE GIFTS!

HARLEQUIN®

American Romance®

Love, Home & Happiness!

YES! Please send me 2 FREE Harlequin® American Romance® novels and my 2 FREE gifts (gifts are worth about $10). After receiving them, if I don't wish to receive any more books, I can return the shipping statement marked "cancel." If I don't cancel, I will receive 4 brand-new novels every month and be billed just $4.24 per book in the U.S. or $4.99 per book in Canada. That's a saving of at least 15% off the cover price! It's quite a bargain! Shipping and handling is just 50¢ per book.* I understand that accepting the 2 free books and gifts places me under no obligation to buy anything. I can always return a shipment and cancel at any time. Even if I never buy another book from Harlequin, the two free books and gifts are mine to keep forever.

154/354 HDN E5LG

Name _____ (PLEASE PRINT) _____

Address _____ Apt. # _____

City _____ State/Prov. _____ Zip/Postal Code _____

Signature (if under 18, a parent or guardian must sign) _____

Mail to the Harlequin Reader Service:
IN U.S.A.: P.O. Box 1867, Buffalo, NY 14240-1867
IN CANADA: P.O. Box 609, Fort Erie, Ontario L2A 5X3

Not valid for current subscribers to Harlequin® American Romance® books.

Want to try two free books from another line?
Call 1-800-873-8635 or visit www.morefreebooks.com.

* Terms and prices subject to change without notice. Prices do not include applicable taxes. N.Y. residents add applicable sales tax. Canadian residents will be charged applicable provincial taxes and GST. Offer not valid in Quebec. This offer is limited to one order per household. All orders subject to approval. Credit or debit balances in a customer's account(s) may be offset by any other outstanding balance owed by or to the customer. Please allow 4 to 6 weeks for delivery. Offer available while quantities last.

Your Privacy: Harlequin is committed to protecting your privacy. Our Privacy Policy is available online at www.eHarlequin.com or upon request from the Reader Service. From time to time we make our lists of customers available to reputable third parties who may have a product or service of interest to you. If you would prefer we not share your name and address, please check here. ☐

Help us get it right—We strive for accurate, respectful and relevant communications. To clarify or modify your communication preferences, visit us at www.ReaderService.com/consumerschoice.

HAR10R

HARLEQUIN®

A *Romance*

FOR EVERY MOOD™

Spotlight on

Classic

Quintessential, modern love stories
that are romance at its finest.

See the next page
to enjoy a sneak peek from
the Harlequin Presents® series.

*Harlequin Presents® is thrilled
to introduce the first installment of
an epic tale of passion and drama by*
USA TODAY *Bestselling Author*
Penny Jordan!

*When buttoned-up Giselle first meets
the devastatingly handsome Saul Parenti,
the heat between them is explosive....*

"LET ME GET THIS STRAIGHT. Are you actually suggesting that I would stoop to that kind of game playing?"

Saul came out from behind his desk and walked toward her. Giselle could smell his hot male scent and it was making her dizzy, igniting a low, dull, pulsing ache that was taking over her whole body.

Giselle defended her suspicions. "You don't want me here."

"No," Saul agreed, "I don't."

And then he did what he had sworn he would not do, cursing himself beneath his breath as he reached for her, pulling her fiercely into his arms and kissing her with all the pent-up fury she had aroused in him from the moment he had first seen her.

Giselle certainly *wanted* to resist him. But the hand she raised to push him away developed a will of its own and was sliding along his bare arm beneath the sleeve of his shirt, and the body that should have been arching away from him was instead melting into him.

Beneath the pressure of his kiss he could feel and taste her gasp of undeniable response to him. He wanted to devour her, take her and drive them both until they were equally satiated—even whilst the anger within him that she should make him feel that way roared and burned its resentment of his need.

She was helpless, Giselle recognized, totally unable to withstand the storm lashing at her, able only to cling to the man who was the cause of it and pray that she would survive.

Somewhere else in the building a door banged. The sound exploded into the sensual tension that had enclosed them, driving them apart. Saul's chest was rising and falling as he fought for control; Giselle's whole body was trembling.

Without a word she turned and ran.

Find out what happens when Saul and Giselle succumb to their irresistible desire in

THE RELUCTANT SURRENDER

Available January 2011 from Harlequin Presents®

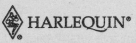

C.C. COBURN
Colorado Cowboy

American Romance's
Men of the West

It had been fifteen years since Luke O'Malley, divorced father of three, last saw his high school sweetheart, Megan Montgomery. Luke is shocked to discover they have a son, Cody, a rebellious teen on his way to juvenile detention. The last thing either of them expected was nuptials. Will these strangers rekindle their love or is the past too far behind them?

**Available January
wherever books are sold.**

"LOVE, HOME & HAPPINESS"

www.eHarlequin.com

har75341

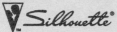

ROMANTIC
SUSPENSE

Sparked by Danger, Fueled by Passion.

Cowboy Deputy
by
CARLA CASSIDY

Following a run of bad luck, including an attack on her grandfather, Edie Tolliver is sure things can't possibly get any worse....

But with the handsome Deputy Grayson on the case will Edie's luck and love life turn a corner?

*Available January 2011
wherever books are sold.*

Love Inspired®

Bestselling author

JILLIAN HART

brings readers another heartwarming story
from

the

GRANGER
FAMILY
RANCH

To fulfill a sick boy's wish, rodeo star Tucker Granger surprises
little Owen in the hospital. And no one is more surprised than
single mother Sierra Baker. But somehow Tucker ropes her heart
and fills it with hope. Hope that this country girl and her son
can lasso the roaming bronc rider into their family forever.

Look for
His Country Girl

*Available January
wherever books are sold.*

www.SteepleHill.com

Steeple
Hill®

LI87643